C000139084

HEAVEN'S A BEACH

HER ANGELS BOOK 2

ERIN BEDFORD

J. A. CIPRIANO

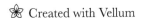

WANT TO GET FREE STUFF?

<u>Sign up here.</u> If you do, I'll send you some free short stories.

Visit Erin on Facebook or on the web at ErinBedford.com.

ALSO BY ERIN BEDFORD

ALSO BY J.A. CIPRIANO

Starcrossed Dragons

Riding Lightning

Grinding Frost

Swallowing Fire

Pounding Earth

The Goddess Harem

The Tiger's Offer

The Wolf's Hunt

The Dragon's War

Justice Squad

Miracle's Touch

Her Angels

Heaven's Embrace

Heaven's A Beach

Heaven's Most Wanted

The Shaman Queen's Harem

Ghosts and Grudges

1

My blood rushed through my veins, my heart beating at a rampant pace. My palms began to sweat, and I quickly rubbed them on my jeans, less my hand slip. My nose had been itching since I'd started, but I refused to jeopardize my mission for the sake of a little itch.

Just a little bit further. I'd never been this close before. Soon, it would be mine. They would all be mine.

"What are you doing?"

I jumped in place, my hand slipping on the keyboard. Right before me, my entire life flashed before my eyes as my last spaceship exploded into a billion pieces. I cried out as the words 'Game Over' appeared on the screen.

Spinning around in my desk chair, I glared up at Lucifer. "You couldn't have waited five minutes? I was almost there! All those hours of hard work, down the drain."

"My apologies, I would never wish to leave you so unsatisfied," Lucifer smirked at me, making my insides tingle most inappropriately. As always, Lucifer stood in a designer suit which fit him like a glove. Today's suit happened to be a sapphire blue that really brought out the color of his eyes, making it even harder to keep my tongue in my mouth and off the floor.

I forced back my attraction to him and stood from my chair. "I'm sure you have left plenty of women unsatisfied." With Lucifer on my tail, I walked toward the little kitchenette area of my new office.

Gotcha! had been up and running for a few weeks now since my first case with the Blessed Falls Police Department, and I had to say business was slow. Okay, not slow. Nonexistent. Sure, I had just started my psychic detective agency, but still, you'd think I'd get a walk-in or even a random crazy spouting tales of alien abductions.

Nope.

The only visitors I've had were kids thinking we

were some kind of joke shop. Maybe Mandy was right, maybe I should change the name. The hundreds of business cards and pens I'd just bought crept up into my mind. Maybe I'd just deal with it.

I grabbed the only coffee mug I had and glanced inside. A few brown stains colored the bottom, but I shrugged and put it under the coffee machine anyway. What? It's my cup!

"I'd never leave you in such a position, love." Lucifer leaned against the counter, his fingers stroking along my arm, causing a buzzing sensation through me. God, what I would give to feel those hands on me for real.

"All talk," I told him pointedly, before snatching my cup of coffee up. Some of it spilled over the side, burning my fingers. Cursing, I sucked on the offended fingers while I kicked the mini fridge open with my foot. Withdrawing my fingers with a loud pop, I set my cup on top of the mini fridge and bent over to retrieve my flavored creamer.

Lucifer made a noise behind me, a mixture of approval and pain. *Good. Let him see what it's like.*

"You know, Jane, I would love to touch you, to make all your dirtiest fantasies come true, but it is you who have been avoiding me, not the other way around." Lucifer's voice had moved closer, and little electrical zips went crazy all over my back. I knew that if I turned around I'd find him pressed up against me, and I couldn't figure out if it would feel even better on my front or not.

Pouring my creamer, I went about mixing my coffee while I tried to think of a plausible answer. Okay, so Lucifer hadn't been avoiding me. Maybe it had been me avoiding him. Or more likely, I got busy and forgot that I had three sexy angels just dying to find out what paradise was really like. And by paradise, I mean my vagina. Believe me, it's wonderful.

I took a large drink of my coffee, closing my eyes and letting out a pleasant hum as the caffeinated sugar hit my veins. Once I had a good buzz going, my eyes snapped open and bored into Lucifer.

"For the record, I never said you were avoiding me, but you could put in a bit more effort. Between working at the bar, consulting for Mandy at the police station, and working here, I'm working three full-time jobs!" I threw a hand up - not the one with coffee, that'd be insane – and I made an overexaggerated exhausted sound. "Really, I can't keep up with it all."

Lucifer tucked his hands into his pockets and

rocked on his heels, his eyes scanning the office. "Yes, I can see you are very busy."

"I am busy," I quipped back, sidestepping him to go back to my desk. I could have walked through him, but all the buzzing energy was conflicting with my caffeine high, and I didn't want to contaminate the experience. I jerked open the desk drawer and pulled out a heavy file, dropping it on the desk so it made a loud plop when it landed. "See, very busy. Lots of cases to solve."

There actually wasn't anything in the folder but a bunch of blank pieces of paper, but he didn't need to know that. For all he knew, I was up to my eyeballs in missing persons and cheating spouses. I could only wish.

"I see," Lucifer mused in that condescending way of his that made me want to kiss him and hit him all at the same time.

A happy thought reminded me that I could do both now. With just a bit of my blood, Lucifer would because a full-blooded angel - eh, person, uh human, thing. I didn't really have the logistics of it all worked out. All I knew was one drop of my blood, and he got to be a real boy! Which, let me tell you, made the whole 'incorporeal to all but me' tortuously good-looking angels so much easier to bear.

Lucifer propped his hip against my desk, traitorously close to my hand. I glanced down at my fingers so close to his delectable ass and then back up to Lucifer, wetting my lips with my tongue. "Yeah, you better see."

Okay, so that was a bit lame but give me a break. I hadn't gotten laid in weeks, and my libido was doing a happy dance at all the deliciousness so close to us.

"Are you sure you don't need a doctor?" Lucifer's brows raised. "You look a bit flushed." He reached out to touch me, and I backed away.

"No, no. I'm fine." I picked up my stack of papers and clacked them on the table. "Just really busy."

"Jane." The way he kept saying my name like it was a prayer or something you would put whipped cream on and lick off each other's body made my nipples stand at attention.

Shooting a glaring 'down, girl' to them, I met Lucifer's gaze. "I'm fine really. Just a bit overwhelmed."

His lips pursed together, his dark eyes peered into me, and I knew he knew I was lying. Of course,

I wasn't alright. I had three, count them three, hotties wanting nothing more than to get jiggy with me. Which I was all onboard for. I wasn't having any 'but there's three of them, I should be true to only one', monogamy bullshit. God handed me three of his tight ass angels, so I was taking what was given. It was the actual taking that was the hard part.

After figuring out that I could make them corporeal, I hadn't really had a good opportunity to make the most of it with Lucifer. I'd already done it with Michael, and Gabriel and I had mostly done it, though I had Mandy to thank for cutting that short. Lucifer was the only one who hadn't gone corporeal yet, and I was having a hard time figuring out how to go about it without making it awkward.

"Jane, you don't have to lie to me," Lucifer purred, that silver tongue of his well at work.

I sat in my chair, my thighs pressing together as I imagined where else he could work his magic tongue. "I'm f-"

"If you say, you're fine one more time, I'm going to tell you horror stories from Hell until your ears bleed." The sharp tone of his voice promptly squashed any dreams of his slippery muscle.

I opened my mouth and then snapped it shut,

shooting him a glare. When he didn't relent, I let out an unattractive grunt. "Geez, you win. I'm not fine. I'm far from fine. I've been working double time trying to help Mandy on her cases as well as work more at the bar to pay for this place."

I waved a hand at me. "I'd hoped to have clients busting down my doors wanting me to help them but have one of them come?" I practically shouted. "No. This?" I picked up the file of papers. "It's just printer paper. It's not a case. It's not anything." I threw it in the air and watched the papers fall around me like rain.

Lucifer sat quietly next to me while I had my meltdown. After a moment, he asked, "Are you finished?"

Glancing around the floor at the mess I made, I grimaced. "Yes. I'm done."

"Good. Then listen to me." Lucifer knelt beside me so that our eyes were level. "You can do this. You didn't get the ability to see us if Father didn't believe you could handle it."

"But why did I get it?" I asked for the millionth time.

Lucifer lifted a shoulder. "Who knows? Father doesn't tell us everything. It's not in his way. Just know that he would never give you more than you can handle."

I gave him a small smile. "I suppose you're right. After all, I think I can more than handle the likes of you."

"Is that so?" Lucifer chuckled, a darkness filling his gaze. "Why don't you prove it?"

With a shy grin, I reached into my desk and pulled out my letter opener. I'd never used the thing, but I was sure happy to have it now. Digging the end of it into my fingertip, I winced.

Red liquid pooled to the top of my skin, and I offered it to Lucifer. Staring up at me beneath his long dark lashes, he dipped his head down until a buzzing feeling spread across my finger. The feeling quickly changed to the warm wet suckling of his mouth as he became corporeal. Even after he became solid, Lucifer didn't stop sucking, and each pull of his mouth was like a lifeline straight to my soaked pussy.

Lucifer's hands slid up my calf and to my parted thighs, his fingers burning through the fabric of my jeans. I scooched forward in my seat, my legs opening wider for him. He released my finger with a languid lick before leaning toward me. I was just about to kiss the Devil when the bell above my door dinged.

"Oh, excuse me!" a female voice exclaimed, and my head jerked up. A poshly dressed woman in her mid-fifties had her hand to her chest and a faint blush on her cheeks.

Pushing Lucifer away, I stood and cleared my throat at the same time I told my raging pussy to shut it down. "I apologize. My associate was just helping me get something out of my eye. I'm Jane Mehr, resident psychic detective." I held my hand out to her with my brightest customer service smile.

The woman took my hand and shook it faintly, her attention more on Lucifer than on me. "No bother at all my dear. I do hope your associate was able to help you."

I chuckled nervously and glanced back at Lucifer who only leaned against my desk with a wicked grin on his face. "Oh, yes, he serviced me really well. I mean, helped me." I stuttered over my words, my own face heating up as Lucifer laughed quietly at me. Trying to regain my composure, I asked the woman, "What can I do for you?"

Giving Lucifer one final look over, the woman turned her attention back to me. "My name is

Daphne Garrett. I was told you were the one to see about unusual cases?"

"Yep, that's me." I grinned so hard my cheeks started to hurt. "Unsolved cases, murders, missing persons. We do it all."

"What about ghosts?" she asked, raising a perfectly coiffed brow.

I stared at her for a moment and then laughed nervously. "Oh yeah. I'm great at ghosts. You could almost say I'm an expert on them." I glanced back at Lucifer who was taking liberties with my coffee.

An expert indeed.

2

"No, it's the maid, she was totally lying about the dishes, I can tell," Lucifer said, glaring at Michael as we stood hiding in the bushes of Mrs. Garrett's mansion.

And I mean mansion.

My parents were well off. My dad was one of the best surgeons in Blessed Falls, and his patients weren't shy with their delight in him. They threw money at him like drunk men threw singles at strippers. My dad was the stripper of surgeons.

A sudden image of my dad in a G-string shaking his thing made me shudder. Yuck.

Stripper surgeon money aside, my parent's house was nothing to laugh at, but Mrs. Garrett's house made ours look like a shack in the middle of the woods. The kind with boarded up windows and no running water. Yeah, that good. They had towels in the guest bathroom you weren't allowed to touch. Believe me, I already got yelled at for it.

Taking my mind off the incident, I turned my attention back to the problem at hand. Mrs. Garrett's ghost wasn't so much a ghost as it was a dirty stinking thief, one we were pretty sure worked for her. The fact that she even thought it was a ghost in the first place made me wonder how trusting this woman actually was. Really, your silver candlesticks don't just go missing. Then again, she did hire me.

"No, Lucifer. It was most definitely the chauffeur." Michael brushed up against me, making my arm buzz. "Can't you tell by how those things were arranged? He definitely rifled through them." Michael crossed his arms over his fuzzy V-neck shirt, looking like a mighty Viking lording over his subjects. His blonde hair fell over his forehead, and his sky-blue eyes were intense and demanding. Even though I had tasted him, just the sight of him still made my skin sing.

"Guys," Gabriel said, looking between them, his button-down Hawaiian shirt flamboyant enough that if he were corporeal, we would have no chance of not being seen. He shoved a hand through his hair and shook his head. "I can't see who they are, but Jane will figure it out. I know it." As he finished speaking, they all turned expectantly to me.

I hated when they did that. I wasn't the brains of this operation. Well, not most of the time. I was the pretty face of the group. They were the ones with all the mysterious powers. There was Lucifer with his built-in lie detector, Michael with his hyper-perception, and Gabriel with visions or whatever. I wasn't quite sure what he did or how it worked. I just hoped he didn't peek into my past. There was a boy band phase I was not particularly proud of.

Powerless and a bit ashamed, I scrambled for an answer. "Um … the butler did it?" I lifted my shoulders sheepishly. Heck, the dog walker might have done it for all I knew.

"Right, of course!" Lucifer exclaimed, far more confident about my answer than I was. "That bloke was definitely lying about something."

"And he's far too messy to make sure to put back things …" Michael mused as his voice trailed off.

Gabriel stared off into the distance for a moment and then nodded. "Yep. He's stolen stuff before."

I frowned. "How can you see that, but not what he's stealing now?"

Lifting a shoulder, Gabriel said, "I don't always get to pick what I see. Sometimes, it's just a glimpse of them now, and other times I get stuff that doesn't matter at all."

Lucifer smirked. "Not that all-seeing, now are you?"

"Lucy …" Michael warned.

"Don't call me that," Lucifer snapped, stepping toward Michael menacingly.

I glanced at the two of them. Michael with his golden coloring and Lucifer with his black hair and seductive eyes, they were like light and dark. Good and evil. Top and bottom. With me preferably in the middle. A Jane and angel sandwich. Now, that was something I could get on top of, or rather in between.

I'm such a weirdo.

Gabriel snort-laughed, making me think he heard my thoughts, but he was staring at Michael and Lucifer. "Just kiss already, you idiots."

My mouth dropped open and my gaze shot back to the glowering angels. "Is … um, is that something you guys do? I mean, kiss each other?" I wrung my hands in front of me, a nervous excitement making me hum with energy.

Lucifer turned to me with a bemused grin. "Would that be something you would be interested in? To see us kiss?"

"I'm not kissing you," Michael snapped, not even looking my way. "The Four Horsemen couldn't make me kiss you."

"We're not talking about the Apocalypse." Lucifer rolled his eyes. "We're talking about Jane." He gestured toward me. "You're saying you wouldn't do that for her?"

Michael finally laid his gaze on me, and he really seemed to think about it. "Well, I'm not sure."

"Don't worry, I'm not asking you to kiss Lucifer, I'd be just as happy if you kissed Gabriel." When Michael's eyes widened, I couldn't hold back my laughter any longer. Laughing so hard my sides hurt, I almost missed the front door opening.

"Look!" I pointed at the butler as he opened the front door. "He has Mr. Garrett's watch on his wrist. It had to have been him."

All three of the angels turned their heads at once to where I was pointing. The butler, Bart Milton, was an elderly fellow, older than my father for sure. Except he had all the class of a shoe horn, not that he knew that. The two times I'd talked to him, he'd had his nose so high in the air that his boogers and I were on a first name basis.

"Maybe they gave it to him and forgot about it?" Gabriel offered as we moved closer to the edge of the bush.

We'd been waiting there for over an hour already, hoping to catch someone in the act of stealing. So far it had been a bust, but I figured the thief wouldn't wear anything they stole while the owners were home. Mister and Misses Garrett had left for the evening, some benefit for one-legged dogs or something.

Rich people were always spending money on some charity or another, but I ask you this, where was that money really going? I didn't see any bionic legs on these poor creatures. All I've seen was rich people getting even richer and poor one-legged Fido was left in the ditch.

"Jane!" Michael's voice knocked me out of my thoughts. "Aren't you going to go after him? He's leaving."

I watched Bart head toward his car at a snail's pace. "Yeah. He's going to get away with how fast he's moving, I better hustle." I scoffed and rolled my eyes. I didn't move from my spot in the bushes as Bart entered his car and pulled out of the driveway.

"Now, you definitely aren't catching him," Gabriel announced, his brow furrowed. "I don't think you're fast enough to catch a car."

"You apparently haven't seen me chase the ice cream truck down before," I quipped as I stepped out of the bushes and toward the front door. I didn't bother trying the doorknob, the butler was good at his job even if he did have sticky fingers. He wouldn't have left the door unlocked. Instead, I knelt next to the door and searched for the hide-a-key I had seen Mrs. Garrett use earlier that day.

"What are you doing?" Michael asked, coming up behind me.

"Yeah, I don't think you're going to find the thief in there, love," Lucifer chuckled.

"I'm not. I'm just looking for … ah hah!" I grabbed the little hollow fake rock and stood. Popping it open, I pulled the key out and turned to show them before using it to open the door. "Voila! Now, we can go snoop in Bart's room to find the stolen items."

"See? Told you she'd figure it out." Gabriel pushed between Lucifer and Michael and followed me into the house.

As we made our way toward the servant's quarters … Yeah, I know. Servants quarters? Who even had those? Okay, Beatrice didn't count. She's not a servant, she's part of the family.

"Don't touch anything," I said over my shoulder, sidestepping a decorative table. "We don't want them knowing we were in here."

"Couldn't even if I tried, love," Lucifer reminded me.

Stopping at Bart's bedroom door, I giggled. "Oh, yeah. Duh. Well, just stand there and look pretty then." I winked and opened Bart's door. Flicking on the light, I went straight to his dresser and started digging through the drawers.

Gabriel leaned against the wall by the dresser. "I thought you said not to touch anything."

I glanced up at him from where I was digging and gave him a pointed look. "Really? How else am I going to find the stolen stuff if I don't touch anything? I meant out there." I waved a hand to the door. "Mrs. Garrett is more uptight than Mandy's butt hole."

Gabriel gave me a strange look which I ignored. He didn't need to know about Mandy's sexual preferences. I didn't even want to know about them, but give my best friend tequila, and all filters go out the door. Really, there are some things you just shouldn't share with others, even your best friend.

I opened the last drawer and dug through the clothes until my fingers wrapped around something. Withdrawing it from the drawer, I blinked at the long purple colored object for a moment and then promptly dropped it with a "Wah!" Backing away quickly from the dresser, I rubbed my hand on my pant leg.

"What was it?" Michael asked, moving toward the dresser.

"Don't!" I reached out. "You don't want to know. Just don't." I rushed forward and kicked the drawer shut with my foot, shuddering as I caught sight of the overly large dildo again. Really, he was, like, seventy!

Lucifer chuckled and grinned at me. I had a feeling he had seen what was in that drawer. Shooting him a warning look, I knelt by the bed. More wary of what I was grabbing, I searched beneath the bed. There was a box tucked a bit further back under the bed. Of course, it was just out of my reach.

I wiggled and stretched trying to reach it, my backside up in the air. Finally, I dropped down to the ground, and shuffled under the bed, grabbing the box. Coming out from under the bed, I smiled at my prize. My grin dropped at the strange looks the angels were giving me. "What?"

Snapping out of whatever haze they were in, Lucifer cleared his throat. "What's that there?"

I shrugged. "Don't know. Hopefully, what we're looking for." I gave them one more curious look before turning back to the box. Pulling the sides of the cardboard box open, my eyes widened. "Jackpot!" I pulled out the silver candlesticks, then the gold-plated picture frame that once sat on the table in the hall, as well as a bunch of jewelry. Grinning up at the guys, I said, "I told you it was the butler!"

"Yes, yes. You are very smart." Michael sighed, his hands on his hips. "Can we leave now?"

"Okay, let me just …" I packed the box back up and shoved it back under the bed.

"You're not going to take it with you?" Gabriel asked, his brows furrowed. "Those are what the client wanted, aren't they?"

"Pfft and tell them what? I snuck into your house and dug through your butler's things." I stood to my feet and brushed off my jeans. "Yeah, right."

"But that's what you did," Michael pointed out as I started for the door.

"Yeah, but that doesn't prove I'm a psychic.

That only proves I'd make a good thief." I shook my head and opened the front door. "Really, guys, you make this job sound hard."

"Ms. Mehr, what are you doing in our house?" Mrs. Garrett cried out. My head whipped toward the door, where she and Mr. Garrett stood dressed to the nines for their benefit.

My mouth dropped open, and I quickly searched for my words. "I … I was just communing with the spirits." I forced a dazed look on my face, my hands moving in the air. "They were telling me who has been taking your things."

"Really?" Mrs. Garrett leaned forward, holding onto her fur throw.

"Of course not," Mr. Garrett - a non-believer if you could believe that - scoffed, jerking a hand at me. "It's obvious she was breaking and entering. So, she's a thief and a fraud."

I dropped my hands slightly and frowned. "I don't like those implications, Mr. Garrett." I stepped closer to him. "If I was a fraud, how would I know about your hide-a-key?" I held the key up for them to see.

"Lucky guess," Mr. Garrett snapped.

"Fine." I threw my brown hair over my shoulder. "Then, if I was a fraud, how would I know that your butler, Bart, is your thief?" I crossed my arms over my chest and stared him down. "How would I know that he has a box of your stuff under his bed right now?"

"He does?" Mrs. Garrett gasped.

"Yep, the candlesticks and the picture frame, plus that necklace your mother left you." I nodded to Mrs. Garrett.

Her hand went to her neck. "Oh, Max. My pearls! I never even told her about the pearls."

Mr. Garrett gave his wife a defeated look before turning a stern look in my direction. "Very well, if you are so sure, why don't you show us?"

"I'd be happy to." I turned on my heel and pushed through the guys. I clenched my teeth and forced myself not to react as I felt like I'd just stuck my finger in a socket. Throwing open the bedroom door, I went to the bed and pulled out the box. "There you are. Your proof."

Mr. Garrett went down on his knees and looked in the box. Sighing in what had to be pure disgust, he glanced back at his wife. "She's right. It's all here."

"Then we should check his whole room, right?" Mrs. Garrett glanced around frantically. "If he took those, there's no telling what else he took."

I backed away from them. "You do that, but I'd avoid the dresser. Your butler is a dirty, dirty man."

With tears in her eyes, Mrs. Garrett suddenly embraced me. "Oh, my dear, I can't thank you enough. How can I repay you?"

I patted her on the back and chuckled nervously. "Uh, a check will be fine."

"Oh yes," Mrs. Garrett pulled away dabbing at the sides of her eyes. "Max, pay the woman and then call the police. They have an arrest to make."

Mrs. Garrett left the room leaving me with her husband. If I thought he didn't like me before, I was sure of it now.

Max pulled out his checkbook from his jacket pocket, filling it out quickly. "You did a good job finding our things. I'm sure this will more than cover your fees and assure you never step foot in our house again." He ripped the check off and handed it to me, his eyes intensely boring into me.

"I can't promise …" I started and then stared down at the check, choking on my words. It was more than I made in three months at the bar. More than even the cops paid me! "Of course, Mr. Garrett. You'll never see me again."

"Good," Mr. Garrett clipped, putting his checkbook back. "Now, get out of my house."

Nodding dumbly, I stumbled out of the room and then out of the house. The guys were still following after me with curious expressions I didn't have the energy to put to rest.

"Where are you going?" Michael asked as I got into my car.

"To get drunk," I said, starting my car. "To get very, very drunk."

3

I had the evening shift at Heavenly Arms, a hole in the wall bar with just the classiest clientele. One of those classy patrons were sitting across from me right now.

"Blech. You call this beer?" Rick, one of our regulars and resident heckler, made a disgusted face before looking to his buddies. How he had any friends, I'd never know. "My grandmother could make better beer, and she's blind and deaf."

"Lucky her," I muttered through clenched teeth.

"What was that, Janey?" Rick asked, turning his beady eyes on me.

Picking up a wet washcloth, I pretended to clean a spot on the counter. "I asked if you needed anything else."

Rick's lips curled up into a wolfish grin, or at least I think it was supposed to be. It seemed more weaselly than wolfish to me. His eyes locked onto the cleavage of my dark green tank top as he leaned forward on the counter. Slicking a hand over his over-produced hair, Rick purred, "You could give me your number and thirty minutes of your time for me to rock your world?"

"Oh, thirty minutes?" I batted my eyelashes at him. "I thought you were more of a one-minute man."

A round of oohs and burns came from his friends. Rick shook off their hands, a frown on his mouth. "Yeah, yeah, laugh all you want. But the ladies always know to come to the Rick-man for the good lovin's. You'll be begging me soon enough."

Begging for a restraining order, more likely. But I kept that comment to myself. One jab was all I was allowed. My boss, Bill, a real-life IT guy if I'd ever seen one, had gotten on to me often enough about busting the drunken asshole's balls.

"Once is enough, but kicking a guy while he's down is downright cruel," he'd said after one particularly pissed-off customer threatened to sue me for verbal assault or some pussy ass thing like that. Not my fault the guy could dish it out but not take it.

Rick, though, was pretty harmless. He was the guy who always hit on you but knew he had no chance in hell of getting anywhere. Which was why I even let the first one out. I knew he wouldn't take it too hard, and I'd only charge him for one beer rather than the three he would down before going to dinner with his buddies.

"I'm sure, Rick," I smirked, handing him another beer. "When that day comes, make sure you record it because no one will believe you otherwise."

His friends ooh'd again but Rick winked at me. "Oh, you know there will be a recording, just not of you begging." He disgustingly licked his lips, and I was done.

Wrinkling my nose, I moved away from him and started down the line of the bar, taking orders and making drinks as I went. After leaving the Garrett's, I had to go straight to work and didn't have a chance to deposit the check burning a hole in my back pocket. I wasn't leaving that thing lying around. It was my ticket out of this shit hole, and I was taking it.

I might not get a lot of clients, but the Garretts made it so that I could finally quit the bartending gig and focus on my psychic detective agency for real. Even if I didn't get another job for the month, I would be okay at least for two. Then I would have to worry about getting another client. I'd get another one by then surely.

At least that was what I was hoping for.

The night was going pretty steadily, boring almost to the point of me hoping the guys would show up. They liked to pop in and out of my life whenever they felt like it. Or whenever God let them off duty. I still wasn't sure about that bit.

There were a few more jerks to deal with after Rick, but most were easily brushed off with a snide remark and a threat to cut them off. Being a week-night, I was the only bartender. Terry, our very own cowboy, had the night off. Piper, our other bartender, only worked the day shift because of having a kid in school. I kind of was glad to be the only one working the bar because that meant I could be alone with Bill at closing. Just the time to tell him I was quitting. I had no doubt that wasn't going to go over well.

"Hey, girlie, can I get a Jack and coke over here?"

I turned with a big grin the one voicing their request instantly familiar. "Why Detective Steven-son, aren't you out past your bedtime? And on a school night too!" I gasped in mock horror, my hand on my chest.

Amanda Stevenson, or Mandy to anyone who really knew her, had only recently been promoted to detective and had been my best friend since elementary school. It was no surprise to see all the males turn a bit toward her. With her honey blonde hair and athletic figure, she could pull even the holiest man's eye. The hoe knew it too.

"I'm here on official business." Mandy lifted her badge and set it on the counter making me grin.

"And official business calls for Jack and coke?" I quirked a brow but made the drink for her anyway.

"Always," Mandy giggled. She took the tumbler from me and took a large swig of it.

"Hard day?" I asked, pouring her another one.

"Well, we've got several high-profile cases that are going nowhere. We are fighting the FBI for jurisdiction on a murder and then there are a string of reports about stolen goods up at Blessed Falls Spa Resort."

"You mean the one by the beach?" I asked, a bit more eager than I should have been at the prospect of laying out in the sun. I really needed a vacation and soon.

"Yeah." Mandy nodded, taking another drink.

She licked her lips, and I swore the whole male population shifted in their seats just now. "Plus, Detective O'Connor is riding my ass about," - she snorted - "well, everything."

"He really needs to see a counselor or something." I shook my head and sighed. "Is he still hung up on his ex-wife? I thought that was done and finalized?"

Mandy nodded. "It is, that's why he's all pissy. Plus, he's had a bunch of complaints about him being overly aggressive with our suspects. The captain is one second from suspending his ass."

"Well, if he's not doing his job, isn't that a good thing?" I cocked my head to the side. Someone hollered at me from the other end of the bar, and I held my hand up to say one second.

"Not with the cases we have on us right now. I need him." She shook her head and shook the ice in her glass.

I started to say something else, but the woman yelled again. Sighing, I told Mandy to hold on. I hurried over to the woman and got her another light beer before hustling back to Mandy.

"Okay, so Detective O'Connor is kind of broken right now. It happens." I shrugged. "What can I do to help?"

"Find my killer and thief," she said, grinning over the rim of her glass.

I leaned my hands on the counter and nodded. "Okay. I don't have experience with killers, but I can help you with your thief. I've gotten pretty good at robberies as of late. I just solved one today."

"The Garretts?" Mandy raised a brow, surprise on her face. "That was you?"

I nodded. "Yep. The butler is one nasty old man, I can tell you that."

"And did your …" She glanced around and lowered her voice. "… angels help you?"

I lifted a shoulder. "Some, but mostly this one was on me."

"Now, that's hardly true." I jumped and glared over my shoulder at Lucifer. "We helped more than a little."

"Is one of them here now?" Mandy asked, leaning forward even more, her eyes darting behind me.

"Yeah," I sighed. "Lucifer."

"What's he saying?" she asked, her head tilting to the side. She was far less scared of my abilities now and more curious. I preferred it that way. I'd rather her ask me a million questions than having to watch what I said around her. Hard to be best friends when you have to keep half of yourself hidden away.

"He's just being himself." I glanced behind me with a wink. "Don't worry about him. The whole of Hell to rule over and he'd rather spend his time in this piece of crap bar."

Lucifer crossed his arms over his chest and smirked as his eyes settled on my short skirt. "The view in Hell does not compare."

I bit my bottom lip and lowered my lashes, a flush spreading across my face as blood pooled in my pulsating clit. Mandy cleared her throat, and I turned my gaze back to her, my face heating even more.

"Sorry, things have been a bit ..." I trailed off as Lucifer moved into my line of view once more.

"I get it." Mandy smiled broadly. "If I had three guys who looked like the one I saw, then I wouldn't even bother putting my clothes back on."

"Believe me. It's a challenge." I giggled and ducked my head once more.

"Well, then you have more self-restraint than me." Mandy laughed with me and then finished off her drink and stood. "I better get going. Like I said, I'm still on duty. If you want to come to the station tomorrow, I'll get you up to speed on the Spa thefts, and then we can see about getting you on as a consultant."

"Sounds good." I took the glass from the counter and sat it in the sink. There were only another few hours left before we closed, and I was counting down the minutes. Especially with Lucifer still there, everything was that much more desperate.

The Devil wasn't making it any easier either. He kept looking at me with those bedroom eyes, his fingers brushing along my skin sending a buzzing through my body every time I passed by him. It took everything in me not to say fuck it all and drag him into the bathroom for a quickie.

By the time the last person left the bar, I was more than antsy to leave. I almost forgot that I was supposed to be quitting tonight. Mandy coming in and offering me another job had only helped to solidify my decision. It made my footsteps firmer and my back even straighter.

"Bill?" I knocked on his office door. Bill's brown head popped up from his desk, his glasses on the edge of his nose.

"Oh hey, Jane. All closed up?" He pushed his glasses back up where they belonged.

I leaned against the door frame and nodded. "Yeah, the last of the drunks have left the building."

"Good, good." He inclined his head. "Well, I'll see you later then. Unless you wanted me to walk you out?" he asked with a raised brow.

I shook my head. "No, I'm fine. I actually do need to talk to you though." Bill turned in his chair and met my eyes, waiting for me to continue. "I've been thinking. With the work with the police and now my new business, I'm getting pulled a bit thin."

Bill sighed and tapped his fingers on the desk. "Of course, you are. I can't say I'm surprised. I had a feeling this would be coming."

"You did?"

"I might wear glasses, but I'm not blind." Bill snorted. "I knew a girl like you wouldn't stay in a job like this for long. I never understood what you were doing here in the first place."

I tucked my hands into my pockets and moved off the door. "What do you mean by that?"

"You've got several degrees, and you choose to hole up in - let's admit it, Heavenly Arms does not live up to its name. You don't belong here."

"Oh, don't say that." I started and then stopped when he gave me a pointed look. "Okay, it's not the best, but I've really enjoyed working here. I just think it's time for me to move on."

"And I'm saying it's about damn time." Bill smiled and stood. Placing a hand on my shoulder, Bill squeezed it slightly. "You go, fulfill your potential. Don't worry about us. We'll be fine. Well, Terry will be pissed, but he'll get over it."

I chuckled with him and sighed. "Okay. I guess that's it then."

"Looks like, unless there was anything else you wanted to talk about?" he glanced around him for a moment and then leaned in slightly. "Though it seems like you have more than enough people to talk to these days."

Oh crap. He saw me talking to one of the guys. Not surprising. It was bound to happen sometime. All the more reason to get out now.

"Well, come by the office if you ever need my services or, you know, just to say hi." I waved a hand.

"And you don't be a stranger. Just because you don't work here any longer doesn't mean you're not welcome." He patted me on the shoulder once more before waving.

Well. That was easy.

4

Blessed Falls Police Station was bustling with activity when I arrived the next morning. Of course, it could hardly be called morning at eleven a.m. Heck if I'm getting up before ten after a late shift, something I'd never have to do again.

A small part of me was sad that I would never work until three a.m. cleaning up the remnants of the drunken idiots of Blessed Falls. Then again, that part was minuscule, almost nonexistent. Who cared about bars anyway?

In any case, I was happy to be working for myself and, on occasion, the fine police men and women of Blessed Falls. I could really see myself settling into a new routine. One that didn't involve cleaning stale beer off my shoes from the night before. Though, there was that one incident with the yogurt at Gotcha! I didn't really want to think about.

Yogurt and hangovers did not go together. Ever.

"Where are you going?" Gabriel asked, popping out of nowhere to trail along beside me.

"To talk to Mandy about a case," I whispered under my breath. I'd just entered the precinct and hadn't even had a chance to announce my arrival. The receptionist didn't need to see me talking to myself first thing in the morning. That was no way to start a day.

"Oh! We have a case?" His eyes lit up almost as bright as his hot pink shirt with pineapples and palm trees decorating it. It was a good thing he had a great personality - and a nice ass - or I'd never have taken one look at him. It probably helped that he was an incorporeal angel and only I could see him. Still, his choice in clothing baffled me.

Clearing my throat, I nodded tightly before stepping up to the counter. I smoothed my hands over my cream V-neck top and adjusted the belt of my jeans before putting on my best customer service smile. The receptionist was the gatekeeper to all that was good and holy. If you pissed her off, there was nothing but hell to pay.

I should know. I'd done my fair share of pissing people off. It was kind of a trademark of my personality. That and my perfect rack.

"Can I help you?" Smith didn't even look up from her desk, but I could still hear the attitude in her voice. She had no time for me, so I better make it quick, and even then, she had even less time.

"Yeah, uh, Jane Mehr for Detective Stevenson." I laced my fingers in front of me on the counter.

Smith sighed, the aggravation clear that I was taking time out of her precious work day. She pressed a button on the phone and Mandy's voice came over the speakers. "You have a visitor."

"Who is it?" Mandy asked, even I could tell the trepidation in her voice. Smith had put her foot down with her as well.

Rolling her eyes, Smith snapped, "Why don't you come out here and find out?"

"I'll … I'll be right there," Mandy stuttered out before hanging up the phone.

Smith gestured behind me with her pen, still not looking up at me. "You can have a seat over there. She'll be out in a minute."

I glanced back to the bench she pointed to and

was happy to see it free of any teardrop tattooed criminals waiting to be processed. Smacking my lips, I dropped my hands and took a seat. Not more than a second after my butt touched the wood then Mandy came barreling through the door separating the front from the back offices.

"Hey," Mandy reached out and grabbed my arm before I could even get all the way up from my seat. "I was expecting you here several hours ago," she hissed as she practically dragged me through the door.

"What's got your panties in a wad?" I grumbled, jerking my arm from her grasp. I rubbed the spot her fingers had pinched, ignoring her glare. "I worked the night shift. You know I wouldn't get up early even if the zombie apocalypse happened."

"Still, it's almost noon. O'Connor has done nothing but bitch about where you are all morning," Mandy explained as we navigated through the desk toward the back.

"And that's different from any other morning?" I smiled back at Gabriel who chuckled. At least, someone thought I was funny.

Mandy huffed and pushed open the door to a conference room. There were papers scattered all across the table and a large rolling board with pictures pinned to it standing next to a very tense Detective O'Connor. From the back, I could see how a woman might fall for him. Large shoulders, a tapered waist, and not to forget the gun and handcuffs on his belt. That alone would get any girl's motor running.

It wasn't until he turned around my eyes landed on his bright orange and green splattered tie that I cried out. "Oh, my eyes! My eyes!" I covered my face in mock horror.

"Jane," Mandy warned.

"Finally. You kept us waiting long enough," O'Connor growled, not even giving me the decency to acknowledge my insult. Well, we'd see who had the last word.

Keeping my hand up over my eyes, I said, "I need my beauty sleep. If I don't get at least eight hours, I turn into a raging monster."

"Oh, please." O'Connor snapped.

"No, no." I countered, keeping my hand up so I couldn't see anything but my palm. "It's all true. Men cry. Women and children run for their lives. It's all very traumatic. A bit like your tie."

"My tie?" The curiosity in his voice turned to irritation as I assumed he looked down at the atrocity hanging around his neck. "Oh, for the love of God. It's just a tie."

"God does not love that tie." I pointed at him. Or at least, I thought I did.

"Got that right," Gabriel muttered into my ear from the side. Because no one could see it, I rolled my eyes. Like he had any room to talk.

"Jane." Mandy huffed once more. "Put your hand down. We can't show you the case if you can't see."

I shook my head, pressing my lips together tightly. "Nope. Not until the monster has been destroyed."

There was silence for a moment before O'Connor asked, "Is she serious?"

"As the day I was born," I held my other hand up in a three-finger salute even though the question was directed at Mandy.

"I'm sad to say she is," Mandy sighed, and a squeak of a chair made me think she sat down. "O'Connor, do you mind?"

Once more there was silence, and then an aggravated growl and some shuffling before something plopped on the table before me. "There are you satisfied, you prepubescent child?"

I peeked through my fingers to find the

offending tie on the table before me. With a happy smile, I dropped my hand and took a seat next to Mandy. "Very. Now, you were saying something about a robbery?"

O'Connor stared at me and then shook his head. He was actually going to let it go. Wow, they must really be pressed for time. It made me feel somewhat bad about giving him a hard time. Somewhat.

"So, over the last month, there have been a string of robberies at the Blessed Falls Spa Resort." O'Connor pointed out a picture of the spa Mandy had told me about. It was elegant in an over-the-top extravagant kind of way. The exact way I liked my spas. "The manager is beside himself worried that the thefts will lead to bad press for the spa."

"Oh, my goodness! we can't have that." I said in my best southern voice my hand on my chest in mock dismay. "What will they say? What will they do? If pa and ma find out, then there will just be hell to pay, and there goes the farm." I gestured wildly in the air earning me a 'Really?' look from Mandy.

"Are you finished?" O'Connor clipped, not at all amused by my antics.

Folding my hands in front of me on the table, I nodded. "Quite."

"Thank you."

"Go ahead."

"I will."

"Alright then."

"Mehr!" O'Connor snapped, his nostrils flaring violently.

I pretended to zip my lips, forcing back the laugh that threatened to explode. Gabriel didn't have to worry about that. He let it rip from his side of the table, his whole body shaking with it. God, was he a gorgeous specimen.

"Like I was saying." O'Connor glared at me for a moment before continuing. "The manager, Riley Parks, would like us to get this taken care of as quickly and quietly as possible. He doesn't want his elite clientele getting word of the incidents and taking off."

I snorted. "Of course not. They go there to relax and get away from the riff-raff, not get ripped off." I sniffed as if I were one of them and then asked, "So, when do I leave?"

"Jane." Mandy knocked on the table, getting my attention. "We need to know you are going to take this seriously. We aren't sending you up there to go on vacation. We're sending you there to catch a thief. A really good one."

I waved a hand in the air. "Pfft. Catching thieves is my thang! I'll have your thief and still get in a nice tan." I stroked my arms, just imagining the golden hue I'd have by the end of this.

"Anyway," O'Connor raised his voice, killing my pre-tan buzz, "the thief is taking things right from the safes. No broken locks. No witnesses."

"It's the manager," I quickly decided with a confident smile.

O'Connor's mouth dropped open briefly before he snapped it closed his bushy brows coming together in joyous union. "It's not the manager."

"Sure, it is." I leaned back in my chair, propping my feet up on the table.

Mandy batted at them, but I didn't drop them. Sighing in defeat, she said, "What makes you think it's the manager? Did you get a vision?" Her eyes moved around the room as if she were trying to see Gabriel.

I shook my head. "Nope. Just look at that guy." I gestured to the photo on the board with the sticky note below it labeling him as the manager. "Just look at that weaselly face and that mustache. No one but a villain has that kind of mustache."

Mandy and O'Connor turned to look at the photo of Riley Parks. I wasn't lying when I said he looked weaselly. He had a receding hairline, leaving only the hair on the sides. His eyes were squinty and too close together. Plus, a panhandle mustache? What, are we in a black and white cartoon?

Mandy scoffed. "That's what you are basing your decision on? His looks?"

I pointed a finger at her. "Hey, don't knock it. I knew that Chuck Barry was a bad guy just from one look, and he ended up cheating on you with Brittany Cormac."

Mandy flushed and glanced back at O'Connor before leaning toward me to hiss. "That was different. This is not high school, and Chuck had a reputation for cheating. You don't need to be psychic to figure out he's bad news."

"Still, you should have more respect for yourself," O'Connor commented, earning him a glare from Mandy. O'Connor cleared his throat and turned back to me. "In any case, Stevenson is right. Unless you have some hard evidence …" I opened my mouth to say something, but he cut me off. "… the kind that can hold up in court. We can't arrest the manager."

"Fine." I pouted, crossing my arms over my chest.

Ignoring my temper tantrum, O'Connor went back to the board. "Our bet is that the culprit is someone who works there, but with us fighting the FBI over this homicide case, we unfortunately need to bring in outside help. Which is where you come in." He didn't even try to hide his disdain about hiring me, which made it that much more exhilarating.

"Great." I snapped my fingers and jumped to my feet. "Just point me in the direction of the massage table, I mean, bad guy, and I'm on it."

O'Connor glared at me. "You are there on the city's dime, and that means, in no uncertain terms, are you to spend it like your daddy's credit card. You get in, make with your voodoo, and get out." He tucked his hands into his pockets and leaned forward slightly. "Are we clear?"

I held my hands up defensively. "Crystal."

"Good." O'Connor turned away from me to look at the board.

"What do you mean by no uncertain terms?" I asked, holding my finger up. "Because there are plenty of terms that I would qualify as certain. I mean, a mud wrap would definitely be something I would think is uncertain 'cause you could get stuff all up in your—"

Before O'Connor could boil over and kill me, probably what he did to his other four wives, Mandy grabbed my arm and pushed me out of the room.

"What?" I whined, taking my arm from Mandy. "I just wanted to be clear on what counted as uncertain terms."

"No, you weren't." Mandy shook her head. "You were being obnoxious. I don't need O'Connor more hyped up than he already is. Just get in there, do the job, and get out. Got it?"

"Aye aye, *Mon Capitan*." I saluted her with two fingers, earning me an eye roll.

"Yeah, yeah. Get out of here. I'll send the files we have to your room at the spa." She started to leave and then paused, putting her hand on my shoulders. "I'm counting on you, Jane. This is your chance to prove you are more than just some parlor trick act. You do this, and there will be a lot more cases coming your way."

I placed my hands on top of hers and smiled. "You can count on me. I won't let you down."

"Good." She patted my hands before releasing me.

"Now to go shopping for the perfect spa disguise." I winked and walked toward the door, leaving a gaping Mandy.

"Is there really a need for a disguise?" Gabriel asked when we got outside.

"No," I said. "But I'll just charge it as a business expense." I grinned, getting into my car. Besides, the city is paying for it."

5

Gabriel wasn't interested in going shopping with me after he found out I wasn't going to buy a new bathing suit. Not that I blamed him. Shopping wasn't my favorite activity. It wasn't even on my list of top ten favorites and one of those was getting drunk with my mother.

Which for all cases and points was a ball of a time, let me tell you. Penny Mehr could get her drink on. But she also over shared … a lot. I did not need to know how my mother lost her virginity at fifteen to her senior boyfriend. Yuck. Some things were better left unsaid.

"You seem peppier than usual," Lucifer said when I entered my apartment.

Setting my bags on the kitchen counter, I smiled at the Devil, who was looking scrumptious as ever. His dark hair was styled so that it had this playful sort of tousle to it, it made me want to run my fingers through it just to mess it up. His suit today was a dark blue with white pin stripes. The white shirt beneath clung to his chest, reminding me of the muscles that lay beneath it. He tucked his hands into his pockets, grinning like a fiend.

It was strange how he so easily looked like he belonged in my apartment. I rarely had all three of them in there at once. It was small enough as it was without me worrying about walking into any of them. I was sure the feeling in my nerves was getting damaged somehow. One could only take so much numbing tingles that didn't come from a vibrator. Which reminded me I needed more batteries.

"Why shouldn't I be? I have some fancy new clothes for my trip to the Blessed Falls Spa Resort, all paid for by the good people of Blessed Falls." I patted my bags on the counter. I wasn't one for shopping but this time I had fun. Probably because I wasn't paying for it.

Lucifer lifted a brow. "I'm sure something in

there made sense, but I'm sorry I'm at a bit of a loss."

Grinning at the adorableness of a clueless Devil, I pulled out a pale blue dress that I knew, from trying it on at the store, hugged my hips and made me look like a million bucks. It better for how much it cost. Thank you, credit card.

"Well, that's lovely," Lucifer drew out, rubbing his chin. "Are you going somewhere special?"

"No, this is my laying around the house dress." I laid the dress on my arm and shook my head, sarcasm dripping from my words. "We have a new case."

Lucifer's lips curled up into a salacious grin. "Well, it is a great dress, but I can't help but think how much better it will look on the floor after I take it off you."

My pulse raced at the heat in his eyes. Suddenly, I was excited for a whole other reason. Setting the dress back down with the rest of the day's goodies, I moved through my small kitchen to where Lucifer stood.

Licking my lips, I looked him up and down taking in the way his suit hugged his form. Really, where did he come up with these outfits? Any of them? Did they subscribe to some kind of magazine, each of them picking one person to model their look after? If so, I'd like to interject some swimwear in there. Maybe something in a spandex form.

Just the thought of the three of them oiled up and in barely anything ... scratch that, change it to absolutely nothing ... Though I'd only seen one of them naked, I was pretty sure that all three of them were built like Adonises. No need to worry about being disappointed in any aspect.

Lucifer's gaze dropped down to the dip in my shirt. "So, is this a case that needs to be addressed at this very moment?"

"No," I breathed. "Mandy is going to text me my information and when I should head over."

"And your other job?" Lucifer's lip curled up at the edge, flashing his canines.

"I ... I quit. Last night." I started to reach out to him, but when my fingertips began to tingle, I remembered our little handicap.

"Do you mind?" Lucifer asked, glancing down at my fingers. "Unless ... you don't want to?"

My eyes widened. "Oh, no. I want to. Believe me, I want to." I chuckled nervously. I searched around for something to prick my finger or cut open a vein, anything to get my hands on the piece of angelic deliciousness so close but so far away from me.

When I couldn't find anything right away, I almost cried. Damn me for not having pierced ears. Or being too safety conscious.

Eventually, I dug into my cutlery drawer and found a knife. Staring at the sharp end of the utensil and then back to where Lucifer stood, I hesitated. I wanted him, I did, but was I really willing to cut myself open for a few minutes of orgasmic bliss?

The way Lucifer looked at me like he wanted to eat me whole answered it for me. Yes. Yes, I was.

I tried not to think about it as I pressed the tip of the blade into the tip of my finger. Red swelled from my skin, and I dropped the knife on the counter and turned to hurry back to Lucifer but gasped when I found him standing right behind me.

"Hey," I held my hand up between us, my eyes darting from the blood bubbling up to the angel across from me. Without a word, Lucifer dipped his head down and wrapped his mouth around my finger, going all the way down to the knuckle. The tingling from his mouth soon warped to a hot wet suction.

Unlike at the office, Lucifer didn't waste any time teasing me. His hands went to my hair, and soon after, that mouth around my finger was on my lips. My hands clenched into fists, twisting with the front of his suit in my grip, pulling him as close to me as possible.

Out of all the angels I'd kissed, Lucifer had to be the most proficient. His tongue stroked mine in a rhythmic pattern as if he were playing my mouth like a violin. Each slide of his tongue caused a different kind of tingle to roll through my body, settling deep between my thighs.

I shoved my hands underneath his jacket, hoping to get closer to the muscle beneath. Lucifer shrugged out of his jacket, his hands dropping from my hair to drag my shirt up exposing my stomach. I lifted my arms up allowing him to pull my shirt up and over my head. My bra came next as did his shirt. We stumbled from the kitchen and across my studio apartment to my bed.

"I've waited so long for this day," Lucifer murmured, his mouth coasting over my skin, and I arched into it. His tongue wrapped around my nipple pulling it into his mouth, making me moan. My fingers curling into his dark locks, I brought him up from my chest to meet my mouth.

My hands met the material of his shirt, and I frowned. Too many clothes. He had too many clothes on. I started to unbutton his shirt, my mouth's preoccupation with Lucifer's making it a slow, grueling process. Jerking my mouth away from his, I grinned at him before grabbing the sides of his shirt and pulling as hard as I could.

"Well, well." Lucifer grinned down at me. "A bit impatient, are we?"

Letting out a giggle, I breathed out, "You have no idea." I grabbed the back of his head and dragged him back down to my mouth. His bare chest brushed against mine, causing all kinds of delightful zings to shoot through me, all of them pooling in my rapidly moistening panties.

Lucifer breathed in deeply. My eyes fluttered open to see the hot desire in his eyes. I barely had a moment to register what was going on before he had my pants undone and tossed to the side along with my soaked panties.

"Have you done this before?" I teased with a raised brow.

"Not with anyone like you," Lucifer replied, pressing his lips to mine briefly before working on his own pants. "No one is like you."

"I don't know if I should be insulted or flattered," I murmured as my eyes trailed down his chest. My fingers splayed over the muscles there as they trailed down to the lines along his hips. The man was utter perfection. Not surprising, considering where he came from.

"Neither." Lucifer grinned wolfishly, his pants thoroughly discarded. My gaze immediately went lower to where he stood proudly, all warm, hard, and ready. Before I knew it, I had it in my grasp and my name on Lucifer's lips.

"What should I be then?" I asked, moving my hand up and down his length.

"You," Lucifer gasped as I tugged on him with a particularly tight grip. "Just be you."

Grinning like a mad woman, I said, "That I can do."

There was no more talking after that, Lucifer made sure of it. His mouth ravaged mine, the slow, meticulous movement from before gone. Apparently, Lucifer wasn't so put together when mad with desire, something I wasn't complaining about. Not one bit.

Lucifer's cock bumped against my folds as we moved against each other. Not quite ready to move to the main event, but too impatient to keep our hands to ourselves. Lucifer worshiped my body like I was his new-found religion and I knew I would have marks in the morning. However, the thought of the Devil branding me like his didn't quite have the dreaded feeling it should have.

I wanted everyone to see the evidence of our lovemaking, to know that I had Lucifer, the number one fallen angel, in my bed. Even if it was for one night. One night I hoped to put on repeat indefinitely.

When Lucifer pressed inside of me, it was like something clicked in my brain. Any kind of resistance I had to the guys was promptly demolished. I knew at that moment, I was supposed to be here. That I was meant to have this power. This ability to bring them into this plane, to give them a taste of what it was like to be human.

Why I hadn't felt it with Michael, I didn't know, but I knew that whatever the reason behind it, I wasn't going to fight it. Not that I could. It felt too damn good to stop, even if I wanted to. Which I didn't. Oh God, did I not want it to stop.

My eyes squeezed shut, and my head fell back on the pillow beneath me as my orgasm ripped through me. Two weeks of pent-up sexual tension and I was close to blacking out from my release. There was nothing in the world like having the Devil between your thighs.

I snort-laughed at that thought as I came down from my high.

"What is it?" Lucifer asked, settling in next to me.

Smiling, I turned to him. "So, Mandy's Catholic. Or at least somewhat."

"Okay?" Lucifer peered at me, his hand stroking my bare shoulder.

I shifted on the bed and leaned onto my elbow. "Well, I was just thinking that there was nothing better than having you between my legs and then that got me thinking about the nuns."

"The nuns?" What could only be described as a devilish grin spread across his lips. "What could those poor ladies have to do with it?"

I couldn't help but smile back at him. "I was just thinking that if they heard the thoughts that I was having about the Devil right this second, they might fall over and die."

Lucifer laughed a full-throated laugh, making my insides clench low. "Sometimes, your mind is a miraculous thing."

"I know." I sniffed, mockingly brushing my shoulder off before collapsing back on the bed. We laid there for a few moments, Lucifer playing with my hair and me contemplating another go, when my phone chirped.

"Don't get it," Lucifer pleaded with me as I tried to get up from the bed. "Stay with me."

I smiled at him. "I wish I could, but it might be Mandy, and like I said, we have a case. With my one stable paycheck gone, I have to make ends meet." Leaning over, I pressed my lips to his but found myself dragged back into the bed and beneath him before I knew it.

"You play dirty," I gasped as his finger found my wet center.

Lucifer smirked. "I'm the Devil, what did you expect?"

I gasped and moaned before replying, "Everything and more." While my phone chirped at me from the kitchen, I let Lucifer drive me into oblivion once more. After all, it was good to have friends in low places. Very low places.

6

W hen Lucifer lost his corporeal form - the people of the world wept at that - I finally went and checked my phone. Mandy had messaged me with the information I needed to head out to the resort.

I didn't bother taking the tags off my new clothes as I shoved them into my suitcase. It was pretty beaten up since I never bothered to buy anything new. The dark green canvas material had faded to a dingy brown. If I'd remembered my less-than-luxurious bags, I would have sprung for new ones while I was out. As it was, I didn't have time now. I just had to hope no one saw me come in. Didn't want to break my cover as one of the rich elite before I even checked in.

"How long will you be at this resort?" Lucifer asked from the bed. Of course, he hadn't bothered to put his clothes back on. They now lay scattered around my room where he'd discarded them, while he lay naked as the day he was born or, well, created, however that worked.

"I don't know." I shrugged, my eyes lingering on his bare form every time I passed by. "Could you put some clothes on?"

Lucifer grinned. "Does my form displease you?" He trailed a hand down his side to lay it on his hip, my eyes followed the movement drawing my attention to his hardening cock.

A bit breathless and more than a little wet, I shook my head. "No, but it does make it hard to get anything productive done, and the longer I have to work, the less time we have to do other things …"

With a bit of a pout, Lucifer conceded. "Very well." Without a word or so much as a snap of his fingers, he was clothed in the same exact outfit sitting on my floor.

"Neat trick," I commented, shoving yet another pair of shoes into my bag. "I could think of a few ways that could come in handy."

Lucifer lifted one elegant shoulder. "I wear them because they are expected of me, not because

I enjoy them. Being attached to material things is a human trait I am happy to not partake in."

I scoffed. "Oh, okay, Mr. Three Piece Designer Suits. Admit it. Looking good matters to you."

Shifting on the bed so that he was closer to me, Lucifer said, "I never said that. Looking good and being attached to one's clothing are two separate things. Besides, who has ever heard of a sloppy Devil?" He flashed me a full-toothed grin.

Rolling my eyes at his arrogance, I finished packing my bag and tried to shut it. No such luck. The bag too small and the number of items in it too many. With a disheartened sigh, I sat on top of the bag and struggled to get it zipped closed.

"Is this a human custom?"

"What?" I asked, still struggling to get the bag shut.

"To sit on one's luggage? Do all humans do this?" His brows rose up on his forehead to create a look of utter fascination with my actions.

"Nope," I breathed, finally getting the zipper half way. "Just broke ones who packed too much to fit."

Lucifer quieted for a moment before asking, "Why don't you just take something out?"

I gaped at him. "But I need all this. I can't just

take something out. That's like asking God to only make animals with legs. Or ice cream without chocolate syrup." I grunted and groaned until I finally got the zipper all the way closed. When I was done, I jumped off the bag and leveled a stare at Lucifer. "It's just unheard of."

He smiled and shook his head. "See, you're attached. That's one of the things I do not understand about you humans. All these things, these bits and baubles, you claim you must have won't give you what you really want."

"And what's that?" I asked, my hands on my hips in a defiant stance.

"Love," Lucifer stated, standing from the bed. "Acceptance. And above all, forgiveness."

"Forgiveness? For what?" I snorted, looking up at him. Man, he was tall.

Lucifer's hand trailed along the side of my face, causing tingles to ripple through me. "All humans, whether they like it or not, have guilt. For something they did or said. Some part of them will always feel guilty for the things they cannot take back. This alone will create their own personal hell."

I hummed, thinking on his words and then sighed. "Well, as thrilling as this physiological debate is, I really need to get going. Mandy will start blowing my phone up at any moment."

"You feel it too, you know," Lucifer continued as if I hadn't spoken.

"Feel what?" I grabbed the handle of my bag and almost pulled my arm out of its socket getting it off the bed.

"Feel guilty."

I chuckled and grunted. "The only thing I regret is not having you put my bag in my car before we had sex."

Lucifer's laugh slithered down my back, not making the bag any lighter. Setting the bag down briefly, I shoved my phone into my pocket and grabbed my purse before opening the door.

"Don't you think you should change?"

I paused at Lucifer's words, glancing down at my clothes. I'd pulled my clothes from before back on and dragged my dark hair into a ponytail. I didn't see why I should change. I hadn't gotten dirty. A naughty thought crossed my mind. At least my clothes didn't.

"What's wrong with what I'm wearing?"

Lucifer leaned against the counter his eyes appraising me. "Well, if you're supposed to be blending in with the socialites, I'm not sure jeans and a t-shirt is the way to go."

Frowning at his words, I realized he was right. Showing up with a shitty bag was one thing, but showing up with a shitty bag and a crap outfit? Unheard of.

I glanced down at my bag, the sides bulging in an effort to contain my stuff. "Fuck!"

I shut the door and dropped to my knees by the bag. Unzipping it more violently than I meant to, I pulled out the first thing I found which so happened to be a red fitted blouse and a thong. Okay, I knew elite were flashy, but I didn't think they would go that far as to arrive without pants. Sticking my hand back into the bag, I searched around until I found a pair of light tan pants and a pair of black heels. They'd have to do.

After changing into my outfit, I spent another five minutes fighting to close my bag again. Heaving and slightly sweaty, I got my bag down the stairs and into my car. Staring at a stain in the passenger seat where I had once dumped a whole blue ICEE, I realized my car wouldn't cut it either. All they had to do was take one look at my car and know that I didn't belong.

Sadly, there wasn't anything I could do about it.

I didn't have time to go beg to borrow my father's vehicle nor did I have the inclination to do so. I'd just have to hope they wouldn't notice what I pulled up in. Besides, Mandy was no doubt waiting with Detective Sourpuss for my arrival. I didn't think making them wait because I didn't have the right car was a good idea.

Lucifer hadn't followed me into my car which made the trip out of town quiet and boring. Blessed Falls Spa Resort might be named after the town, but it sat twenty minutes out of the city limits. Probably because that was the only place any suitable line of beach sat, something that they quickly monopolized on, leaving the rest of us a tiny public beach that was always packed to the max on sunny days.

Pulling up to the resort, I decided to forego letting the valet park my car and found a nice parking spot near the back. I got out of the car and patted the top lovingly. I loved my car, but some things were better left hidden.

"I'll see you later," I told her after I took my bags from the back. Halfway through the parking lot and I wished I'd chanced using the valet.

"Miss," a teen clad head to toe in white called out as he approached me. "Please let me get your bag." He eagerly reached for the handle of my beat-up suitcase, a sort of grimace on his face when he saw it.

"Sure thing." I grinned broadly, letting him take the heavy bag.

"Your room?" he asked, and I had to pull my phone out to check the text from Mandy.

"125. Ha, not too far off from how much I weigh," I told him with a cheeky grin. He politely smiled in return, but I could tell he didn't mean it. I'd already lost his affection with my trashy bags. No tip for you, bucko.

I searched around the entrance to the spa, looking for Mandy or O'Connor but only found palm trees. Lots and lots of palm trees. Did they not decorate with anything else? Trying to take in everything I could, I moved slowly through the entryway.

Blessed Falls Spa Resort looked every bit as beautiful and luxurious as its brochures — a two-story building with tall columns decorating the front. It had marble statues of scantily clad men and women and a fountain so huge that I could swim in it. The only thing breaking up the Greek sort of theme they were going for was the window-washer cart handing from the building. I hoped that didn't mean I'd have to wear a toga. I didn't mind going commando on occasion, those occasions being for sexy time and getting massaged, but no underwear for the sake of appearances was not my thing.

Stepping into the building, I finally found Mandy's blond head of hair standing next to a dark one and the weaselly man I knew as Riley Parks. Moving through the reception area, my eyes scanned around. The inside held the same kind of Grecian theme except the palm trees were replaced with large vases of multicolored flowers.

"This place is pretty cool," Gabriel's voice spoke up beside me, making me jump in place.

"Yeah, it's nice," I muttered, trying not to pull anyone's attention.

"Is this the case from before?" He followed after me as I headed toward Mandy.

I nodded but didn't answer so close to the others. The manager saw me first and his brows furrowed as if he expected someone else and perhaps a bit of displeasure. Not surprised. No one liked psychics. They all thought we were fakes and cons. Well, I might be the former but definitely not the latter.

When Riley pointed his chin at me, Mandy and

O'Connor turned. O'Connor frowned, not unusual there, but the tense expression on Mandy's face had me worried.

"Hey guys, I hope you didn't start the party without me." I grinned from ear to ear, determined not to let the aura screaming 'you don't belong here' bother me.

"Mehr, it's about time you got here." O'Connor pushed the flaps of his suit jacket back to put his hands on his hips, his gun and badge in full view.

"Should we really be talking out in the open like this?" I asked, gesturing around to the passing spa members. "Won't it give off the wrong impression?"

"We were just leaving," Mandy told me before putting something in my hand. "Here's your I.D. and room key."

I glanced down at the wallet in my hand and opened it up to see a fake I.D. with cards to match. She must have gotten my picture from social media, but the weight and name were way off.

"Hey, I'm not a hundred and thirty pounds!" I cried out with a scowl. "And couldn't you have thought of a better name? What's wrong with using my own?"

O'Connor leaned closer to me, and growled, "Who cares what your weight says, and do you really think these people won't look you up? The moment they find out you're a psychic detective, they will clam up, and nothing short of a lawyer will get them to talk to you."

I sniffed and tucked my wallet into my purse. "You underestimate my abilities. I once charmed the pants off a priest in training during Sunday Mass."

"Not something to be proud of," Mandy retorted crossing her arms over her chest.

"We'll have to agree to disagree," I said to Mandy. To Riley Parks who had been watching this whole time curiously, I held my hand out, "Hello, I don't believe we have met. I'm Patrice Ludmire." I cringed as I said the name out loud. Nope. So not me. "But you can call me Patty. All my friends do."

Riley shook my hand. still displeased by my presence. "Nice to meet you. I think it goes without saying that I want this done as quickly and discreetly as possible. None of my guests should know what you are here for."

Says the man having us meet in the middle of the lobby. Out loud, I said, "Don't worry, Mr. Parks. I will have your resort free of thieves and back to draining the trust funds of our local elites in no time."

Sticking his nose in the air, Riley stiffened. "See that you do." He nodded to Mandy and O'Connor. "Detectives."

I plastered on an over-eager grin and looked at the two. "So, point me in the direction of the beach. I'm ready to get my tan on."

7

After Mandy and O'Connor left with a warning for me not to mess around, I headed up to my room, if you could call it that. Larger than my studio apartment, it could hold two and half of my actual homes in its walls.

I'd expected to get one of the shabbiest rooms of the place, and if this was it, then I half wondered what the others looked like. A kitchenette area sat to one side of the room, the other had a sitting area, and then the bedroom was partially walled off in a semblance of privacy. The moment my eyes landed on the king size bed, I skipped toward it. Jumping onto it, I sank down into the soft comforter with a puff of air. Like sleeping on a cloud.

I closed my eyes briefly, enjoying the bed I

would dream about when I left. I had completely forgotten about Gabriel until a chuckle pulled me from the bed.

"What?" I arched a brow and smiled.

Gabriel leaned against the entryway, his button-up Hawaiian shirt making him look like he belonged here much more than me. His eyes never left my form and twinkled with mischief.

"You find pleasure in the smallest of things."

I shrugged. "Well, you would too if you didn't live forever." I grinned and twirled my finger along the top of the bed. "In fact, I think I could get you to change your tune with a little blood."

A sly grin curled over Gabriel's lips. "Are you trying to seduce me?"

"And what if I am?" I winked, playing with the edges of my shirt.

"I'd say hell yes, but Michael is expecting me back any minute now. I do have a job you know." His words said one thing while his body moved closer to me.

"Oh yeah." I clicked my tongue. "There are so many messages to be delivered. We wouldn't want God to forget to get his hair done."

"You joke, but you don't know the dire conse-quences that come with missing a delivery." Gabriel chuckled. "A whole village flooded once because I wasn't told in time to warn their shaman. It was quite catastrophic."

I let out an exaggerated sigh. "Fine. Go. Save the world, while I roll around on this marshmallow of a bed. Naked." I wagged my eyebrows at him, making him laugh again.

"You do that." Gabriel leaned over the bed and brushed his mouth against mine. The buzzing feeling left my lips feeling numb, but it was the thought that counts.

When I opened my eyes, Gabriel was gone. Sighing again, I let myself lay in the bed a few more minutes before getting up. The bell boy had taken my bag up to my room as instructed, thankfully without any kind of destruction on its part. I had a feeling these workers were the type to spit in your food or use your toothbrush to clean the toilet if you got on their bad side.

I dragged my bag onto the bed and dumped its contents. No need to be all fancy now. No one was looking. I did take a moment to hang up a few items that had already begun to wrinkle at my mistreatment of them. No reason I should look like a complete slob. When that was done, I found my bathing suit and pulled it on. I found a robe with the spa's name and logo on it that felt almost as good as the bed wrapped around me.

"Hello, lovely," I purred as I pulled the collar up around my face. Slipping my room key into the pocket of my robe and grabbing my bag of beach supplies, I headed out the door.

I nodded and smiled at the guests and workers as I passed by them. I wanted to keep up the appearance of actually being there to relax and not on a manhunt. Or womanhunt. Equal rights and all that.

The best way to blend in was to take advantage of the spa itself. I hadn't been lying when I said I wanted to go to the beach. When I worked at the bar, I stayed up late and slept in even later, so going to the beach was a rare treat. Now that I had easy access to it, I would take full advantage of it.

Since it was later in the day, there weren't that many people hanging around the sandy beach. There were a few couples and what looked like a bachelor party, but no families with a bunch of noisy children. Just how I liked it.

The spa had been kind enough to provide lounge chairs with large umbrellas over the top to keep the rays from beating down on you. At the moment, that was all I wanted. I shoved the umbrella aside and plopped my robe down on the chair beside me. I had barely laid down when a cute blonde woman wearing the spa's logo on her white shirt came over.

"Hello, can I get you something from the bar?" The brilliant smile on her face made me feel a bit better about my stay, much more so than the look I'd gotten from the bell boy.

While Mandy and O'Connor would have had a field day about me drinking on the job, I said screw them and ordered a Mai Tai. The blonde whose name tag read Jessica scurried away to fill my order, leaving me to my sun.

My skin started to warm, and I remembered I hadn't put on sunblock. Sighing, I opened my eyes once more and dug through my bag. No one wanted a lobster-colored psychic. Plus, I planned on christening that bed before my stay was through, and I didn't think a sunburn would be all that sexy. No matter how heavenly the company.

I started to rub the banana and coconut scented lotion down my legs and over my arms when a man I didn't know dropped into the seat next to me. I continued to put my sunblock on while I waited for my guest to announce himself. He wasn't unattractive with his windblown brown hair and a smile that reached his eyes. Too bad I'd already tasted heaven, and that had ruined all other men for me.

"Can I help you?" I asked finally, after he did nothing but stare at me. Really, it was beginning to creep me out.

"I'm Mick," he said, simply giving me what he must have thought was a seductive smile. It looked more like he had something in his eye.

"Uh, that's nice." I forced a polite smile in return and finished putting my lotion on just in time for Jessica to return. "Thank you." I took my drink from her and took a large sip before settling back into my chair.

"So, what's your name, beautiful?" Mick was either not the brightest bulb in the batch or just didn't like being blown off. I was going for the former.

"Patrice." I sipped my Mai Tai again, begging the alcohol to kick in fast.

A round of laughter came from the bachelor party, and I peeked over at them. They were pointing and laughing at Mick, who was now getting frustrated.

He threw his legs over the chair of his seat so that he faced me and clasped his hands in front of him. "So, what brings you here?"

Raising a brow at his words because, seriously, this one was not a smooth talker, I tried to find a way to let him down gently without giving him any impressions that I was interested. I should be good at this kind of thing, I used to do it at the bar all the time. Heck, I did it just last night!

Before I could get an answer out though, Lucifer and Michael appeared on either side of Mick. Though he couldn't see them, Mick could feel their presence. His shoulders tensed, and he glanced around nervously, but he didn't back down. Must have money at stake.

"Is this man bothering you?" Michael asked, looming over Mick. I hid my face behind my glass and shook my head.

"You don't know?" This time it was Mick who laughed. "Wait, I'm confused."

"You and me both, brother," I muttered into my drink, my eyes going off to the side. Sitting my drink down, I cleared my throat. "Look, Mike, is it?" I knew his name, but it makes them feel a bit less important if I say the wrong name.

"Mick," he corrected me, a bit more disheartened. Poor guy. I bet this was really hard for him to do. I'd have gone to give his friends, who were still laughing their asses off, a piece of my mind and a foot in the ass if Michael and Lucifer didn't look ready to rip the guy's head off.

"Right, Mick." I looked pointedly at him. "I'm here for work. I don't have time to play with some guy who is just here for the weekend because of some bachelor party."

"How? How did you know that?" He gaped at me and looked back at his friends.

"I'm psychic." I grinned and then added, "And I can tell you now. That this" - I gestured to us - "isn't going anywhere. In fact, your whole weekend is looking pretty slim. I suggest you go back to your friends and worry about making sure your boy walks down the aisle and doesn't get wrapped into playing peek-a-boo with a stripper. Cause this is a waste of both of our time."

Mick looked like he had swallowed something nasty, his skin a green pallor as he stumbled to his feet and walked back to his friends. He kept glancing back at me on his way back, but the look he gave me was more of fear than rejection. Maybe I was closer to the truth than I thought.

When I was once again alone save for the two looming angels, I picked my drink up. Lounging back in my seat, I sipped on my straw staring up at the two of them. The possessive alpha aura they had been exuding seemed to slowly dissipate as their eyes settled on me.

"So, what's up?" I asked, cocking my head to the side. A matching look of confusion covered their faces as their eyes bore into me. I released my straw from the corner of my mouth and touched my cheek. "Do I have something on my face?"

They didn't answer at first, their eyes hot on my skin. Then Michael crossed his arms over his large chest and asked in a low voice, "You do realize you are practically naked in front of all these people?"

My brows furrowed together and then I looked down at myself. The bathing suit I'd chosen, a deep red two-piece with thick straps on the top and bottom, wasn't even as revealing as some of the others on the beach.

Turning my eyes back up to Michael, I chuckled nervously. "You're worried about what I'm wearing? That woman is wearing a thong!" I gestured a hand to a woman in her mid-thirties not too far away from me. "And that one is only a hop away from a nip slip." I pointed at a bouncing beauty that was getting the majority of the bachelor party's attention.

"They are not our concern," Lucifer interjected, his eyes solely on my form. "That man didn't come over here because he liked your hair."

I made a face and then fluffed my brown locks. "What's not to like? It's long and luxurious. Any hair commercial would be happy to have me."

Michael and Lucifer exchanged an equally bewildered look before Michael stepped closer. "Is this a usual occurrence for you? To flaunt yourself to the public?"

I snorted. "Like you're one to talk. If anyone flaunts themselves, it's you guys. There are books, songs, even freaking statues depicting your likeness." I scanned my eyes over his form and winked. "All of your likeness. And here you are getting your panties in a twist because some silly boy decided to try his luck with me."

Michael fumed, his nostrils flaring almost comically. "My panties are not in a twist."

"Oh right." I giggled. "You don't wear anything under those butt-hugging jeans." My eyes moved over to Lucifer. "And you. You're at a freaking beach, and you are wearing a suit! A three-piece fucking suit!" I threw my hands up in the air and shook my head. "And here I thought I was having a good influence on you three. Apparently, Gabriel is the only one who takes notice when I speak."

"You rang?" Gabriel popped up beside Lucifer. His eyes immediately went to my outfit and then where we were. "Oh cool. Are you going to go swimming? Can you do that thing they do on T.V.? That slow running, chest bouncing thing." He put his hands up to his chest, mimicking what he was saying.

"See?" I gestured a hand at Gabriel. "That is an angel acclimated to the human world. Really, you two, I'm disappointed." I shook my head and picked up my sunglasses, perching them on the edge of my nose. "Now, if you don't mind, I have sunbathing to do in my scandalously clad outfit. Shoo." I pushed my glasses up onto my face and laid back on my lounger, not bothering to see if they left. This was my vacation damn it, and I was going to enjoy it!

fter my time at the beach, I clothed myself, chuckling the whole time at Michael and Lucifer's antics. Seriously. They acted like they'd never been to a beach before.

Since the spa was a classy place, I had settled on a green sleeveless dress that clung to my side and sparkled in the light. It was the only dress I had that would expand as I would, and I fully expected to add a few pounds during my time here. Their brochure said they had an epic buffet, and it was just calling my name.

"Hey, there." Gabriel strolled up beside me, his hands in his cargo shorts and a twinkle in his eye. "You look great."

I smoothed my hands over my dress and

grinned. "Thanks. I'm heading to dinner. Want to join me?"

Gabriel's grin expanded but then dropped. "Wait, this isn't going to be like with the hot sauce will it?"

The memory of giving Gabriel hot sauce while he ate his very first human food came to mind. He had thought he was so big and mighty. When he had shoved the huge bite into his mouth he had been in for a big surprise. I still hadn't been able to get any of the others to try it as well. It was something that I knew I had to see before I died.

Giggling at the memory, I shook my head. "No. No hot sauce. Promise."

"Okay, then. Sure."

"Wait," I paused and pointed at his outfit. "You can't wear that."

Frowning, Gabriel glanced down at his colorful Hawaiian shirt and shorts. "Why not?"

I scowled. "Because, this is a classy place. I don't know if they'll even let you in without a suit jacket."

Suddenly, a jacket not unlike one of Lucifer's appeared on Gabriel, the rest of him still clothed like some kind of surfer. A snorting laugh escaped me before I could contain it. Really, I didn't know what was wrong with these guys. You'd think they had some kind of fashion sense in heaven. Unless they were all wearing robes and sandals. Or better yet, no clothes at all. The thought made me grin until I remembered there were female angels as well. They better not be naked, throwing their perfect bodies all over *my* angels.

"What?" Gabriel asked, turning this way and that. "Is this not what you meant?"

I shook my head, my hand over my mouth as I chuckled. "Not quite."

The next blink had me faced with a full suited Gabriel, his brown hair slicked back from his face and a dazzling grin on his lips. "How about now?"

I gaped at him, all the sane thoughts chased from my mind. Swallowing thickly, I nodded like a bauble head. "Yeah, that'll work."

With that settled, I kept walking toward the dining room, but Gabriel didn't follow. Turning on my heel, I looked back at him expectantly, but he simply stared at me. It took me a moment, and then I smacked myself in the forehead.

"Sorry, brain fart." I grinned and sauntered back over to him. I opened my clutch and dug around for something sharp. Tampon. Hair tie. Cell phone. God. Where's a knife or a random safety pin when you needed one?

"Ah hah!" I pulled out a tiny pearl earring that had been wedged in the corner of the bag. Without thinking too much about it, I shoved the sharp end into my finger and held it out to him.

Unlike Lucifer who had made the act of taking my blood as obscene as possible, Gabriel flicked his tongue out to taste the blood bubbling up. The change was instantaneous. Gabriel already had a presence to him, but now that he was solid, the hallway seemed to shrink under the full force of his existence. His very being made my hair stand on end in the best way possible.

God, let this last through dinner.

"Shall we?" Gabriel offered me his arm and a cocky smirk like he knew exactly how he affected me and loved it.

I looped my arm through his and pressed myself closer to him. Warmth filled me through the line of his suit, and I suddenly wasn't thinking about dinner any longer. My only desire was to get Gabriel's clothes off.

Opening my mouth to suggest skipping dinner, I clamped it shut when we moved into a crowd of dinner goers. Too late now.

"Hello, welcome to the Sea Side Buffet. How

many in your party?" The maître d' glanced between us with a curious look.

"Just two," I stuttered out, my eyes searching behind him to the room beyond. Many of those I had seen on the beach were in the dining room as well. Even the bachelor party was there. Mick though didn't seem to be having as much fun as the rest of his group.

Poor guy. I should have been a bit nicer to him, maybe slipped him a nip or something so he'd have a tale to bring back to his friends.

Gabriel squeezed my arm in his, snapping me back to the present. I looked up at him, a feat on its own with the height difference between us. For a moment, I wished I'd chosen to wear the heels I'd packed instead of my flats.

We were ushered into the dining area and toward a table. Unfortunately, that table was right next to another one with a full group of women, all who turned their gazes to Gabriel. *Need a bib for that drooling, ladies?*

Forcing myself to restrain my need to claw their eyes out, I took a seat in the chair Gabriel had pulled out for me. I leaned up and pressed my lips to his before letting him push me in. I might as well have lifted my skirt and pissed on him for as subtle as I was being.

He's mine, bitches.

It was odd, how possessive I felt over Gabriel. I'd never been this way with any of my other boyfriends. I've always been the 'if he wanted to go with another woman then he obviously wasn't for me' type. Not this time though. This time I had something I wanted, and I planned on keeping it.

Never mind the fact that he was an angel and wouldn't stay corporeal for more than an hour or so, but still, who needs rational thoughts like that?

Our waitress came by and took our drink order, all the while the table of four stared at Gabriel. With a tight smile, I reached over and took Gabriel's hand. "I'm so happy you came today. We've hardly spent any time together lately."

Gabriel squeezed my hand in return. "Well, my brothers aren't here to interrupt us, so let's make the most of it." He glanced around the table, his brows furrowing. "Where are the menus?"

I patted his hand and started to stand. "Oh, silly. This isn't that kind of restaurant."

"It's not?"

"It's a buffet. You serve yourself." I gestured toward the line of food set up along the wall. He followed me over to the line, and I handed him a plate. "Here. You put what you want on here, and when you are done, you come back up and get another plate."

"How many times can I do this?"

"As much as you want."

Gabriel's eyes widened, his mouth gaping. We went along the line, and I pointed out different items to him as I piled my plate full. "Also, don't feel like you have to eat everything on your plate. The beauty of a buffet is if you don't like something you got, you can come and get something else."

"That's so awesome." Gabriel grinned, his plate already filled to the brim with a mixture of foods that even I found suspect.

"Okay, let's go." I led the way back to our table, but a commotion behind me made me stop. Turning back around, I found Gabriel with his plate of food held in one hand and one of the women assigned to the table next to us draped over his side.

"Pardon me," she purred, her fingers trailing over Gabriel's chest. "I wasn't watching where I was going."

"No problem." Gabriel grinned. "It could happen to anyone."

The woman didn't give up there. She pressed

herself closer to him and simpered. Yes, simpered. I wanted to yank her off him by the roots of her overbleached hair.

"I'm so lucky to have such a big strong man to catch me. I really appreciate it." She started up on her tiptoes, her mouth close to his ear. "How can I possibly repay you?"

Gabriel, completely oblivious to this woman's come-ons, released her and stared back down at his plate. "You can tell me … how's the lobster? I've never had it before, but I've heard it's quite good."

Gaping at him, the woman stuttered out, "It's okay."

"Great." Gabriel smiled at her once more. "Thanks."

I couldn't help my giggle as he made his way toward me, leaving the woman dejected and confused. And I worried he'd be more interested in one of them? He had eyes only for the food on his plate. The angels didn't seem to know it, but they were more like human males than they wanted to believe.

"So, have you found any clues yet?" Gabriel asked after he'd finished off his fifth plate. They were piling up in front of us at an alarming rate. Most of them were his, but I found his love for food had liberated me into going past my two-plate limit.

Guilt rushed through me at his question. "Actually, I haven't really been doing my job. I've been too caught up in vetting the place out."

"Don't feel too bad about it. You've been working too hard. You should have a little fun." Gabriel stroked his thumb across the side of my mouth, taking some kind of sauce with him before popping that thumb into his mouth. Hot need raced through me, and after having filled my stomach, my other needs were demanding I sate them as well.

"Will you look at that?" a snotty voice asked from the table over. I didn't turn, but my ear peaked at their words. "How did a plain Jane like that get an Adonis like him?"

"I know exactly what you mean." I recognized the blonde woman's voice immediately. "I'd lick every gorgeous inch of him."

"You're so bad." Another woman giggled. "But good luck getting past his guard dog. I swear my bulldog's face isn't even that pudgy."

My hand tightened around my fork, biting into my skin. I was two seconds away from slamming it into the woman's eye when Gabriel spoke.

"You know. It takes a real man to see beyond

just his eyes." This had the women at the table clamming up as Gabriel took my hand gripping the fork. "I never thought I'd find anyone like you in all my existence."

I let out a heavy breath and all my anxiety with it. Gathering up a genuine smile, I stared into Gabriel's eyes. "I feel the same way. You can't imagine how much you've made my life better. Made me feel normal and accepted."

Gabriel moved closer his voice lowered. "There's nothing that needs accepting. You're perfect the way you are." His words made my heart swell, and all my insecurities wash away. "And I know my brothers feel the same way. We never expected all to fall for the same woman."

A collective gasp from the other table made my shoulders tense. My face swiveled slowly from Gabriel to the four women all in a state of horror.

"You hussy," the blond hissed.

"Lucky bitch." Another fanned herself with her napkin.

"Gladys!" one of the others cried out in disgust. "How can you think that?"

Gladys looked at her friend and then gestured to Gabriel. "Well, look at him. If he had brothers, I wouldn't say no to a little ménage a trois action."

A wicked grin crept up my face as I stood. Bringing Gabriel to stand with me, I turned to the women and leaned in as if I had a secret to tell. "Try ménage quatre."

The gasps of horror and envy followed after us as we left the dining room, Gabriel and I laughing all the way.

9

We didn't stop laughing until we reached my room. I fumbled with my key, the giggles making me shake. When I finally got it open, Gabriel and I practically fell in.

"That was hilarious." Gabriel chuckled, leaning up against the kitchenette counter.

I grinned. "Did you see their faces when I implied all have sex together?" I giggled, my hand going to the fridge. "Like that would ever happen."

"You don't think so?" Gabriel asked, his breath suddenly on the back of my neck.

I closed the fridge without actually looking inside and turned around, my face inches from his. "No, I just haven't really thought about it." Lie.

"Besides, Michael and Lucifer are far too alpha male to want to share me at the same time. I'm lucky to get them separately. Wouldn't want to rock that boat. At least, not now."

"And me?" Gabriel's hands circled my waist, pressing me against his hard chest. "Am I not an alpha male, as you say?"

I licked my lips, my mouth suddenly dry. "I wouldn't say that, no, but you have your own kind of strength. One that doesn't quite require all the peacocking."

"Peacocking?" Gabriel cocked a brow. "Is that what you call it?"

I smiled slightly. "Well, that's what they do. Both flaunting themselves, trying to get my attention over the other. If that's not peacocking, then I don't know what is."

One hand came up to cup my chin. "And you don't think I peacock for you?" For some reason, every time he said peacock, I could only focus on the one part of it. Cock. And Gabriel's was hard and pressing into my stomach, making my mind turn to goo.

"I'm not saying that." I leaned into his touch, my eyes closing briefly. "I'm just saying you aren't the kind to make demands on me. Or the others.

Not like they do. You seem more than happy to share me as long as you get a piece of the Jane pie too."

Gabriel smiled slightly, but it wasn't his happy-go-lucky smile. It was one I hadn't seen before. No, this smile was hard with a hint of danger attached to it.

"I'm not as laid back a guy as you think, Jane." The way his said my name caused a shiver to run down my spine, my blood beginning to pulse in anticipation.

"Really?" I breathed out, not able to think of anything else to say. "Then what kind of guy are you?"

Gabriel stroked along my bottom lip before tugging it slightly. "The kind who bides his time." He leaned in until his mouth brushed against mine, just barely hinting at his taste. "I watched and waited, all along making jokes." His mouth pressed to mine again, this time catching my bottom lip between his teeth pulling until it almost hurt. He let it go before lavishing it with his tongue, soothing the ache. "But you see, it's the patient man who really gets the prize."

His mouth covered mine, pinning me between the counter and his body. I had no neurons left shooting in my brain to even comprehend what he said, let alone what was going on. They had long since flown the coop in the face of a serious Gabriel. His lethal tongue took over my mouth, making me groan for more.

My hands grabbed his hair, pulling him closer to me still. The hand holding my face released me to fondle the hem of my dress and then, without warning, it was pulled up and over my head, leaving me in my underwear. I tried to bring Gabriel's face back down to mine, but he pushed me back, forcing me to stay still while his eyes took me in.

"God, you're beautiful," he announced, and I came out of my haze long enough to giggle. "What?"

I covered my mouth with my hand and shook my head, refusing to tell him why I laughed.

Gabriel's eyes narrowed to slits and his arms caged me in against the counter. "Jane." The warning in his voice made my insides twist into sexy knots. "Tell me, or I won't touch you again."

"You're touching me now," I pointed out, his arms brushing against my side.

"You have a smart mouth. Has anyone ever told you that?" Gabriel leaned in close, his mouth just inches from mine.

"All the time," I murmured back, leaning toward him to close the distance, but he pulled back at the last second, making me growl.

"Tell me."

My brow furrowed for a second forgetting what we were even talking about in the first place but then my mouth dropped open as I remembered. "Really? We have so little time together, and you're going to risk not getting to finally have sex over a little giggle?"

Gabriel's gaze didn't waver.

"Ugh, God you are such a …" I trailed over, crossing my arms over my chest and muttering under my breath. Still, Gabriel didn't budge. "Fine! Okay. You win. I giggled because you took the Lord's name in vain."

Gabriel frowned. "I don't get it."

"Of course, you don't." I sighed. "You said 'God, you're beautiful.' For a regular person, that'd be all fine and dandy but for you, it could mean several things. You could be saying 'God, you're so beautiful,' and mean God actually. Cause you know, he's your dad and all."

Gabriel's face scrunched up even more by my explanation, but I wasn't even done yet. "Or you could actually mean, 'God, you're so beautiful,' in reference to me, but in that case, it means you are using his name in vain, which in turn could get you in trouble. And then I thought your dad would give you a spanking, which in of itself ended up in a very naughty, weird place." I threw my hands up and grabbed my hair. "I'm such a freak."

He didn't say anything at first, only stared at me. Which only made it all the worse. I jiggled my leg in place and grabbed his arms. "Please, just say something. I'm dying here."

The downturn of Gabriel's mouth slowly moved upward in a grin as he shook his head. "You are something else, Jane Mehr. Truly something."

"Is that a good thing or a bad thing?" I asked, still very anxious about his reaction to my weird brain patterns.

"I think …" Gabriel shrugged out of his jacket and set it on the counter. His hands moved to the buttons of his shirt. First the cufflinks and then the front, his tie loosened and discarded. "It's a very good thing." He leaned in once more, his mouth skimming mine. "In fact, it's so good, I don't think I can spend another moment without finding out every strange and obscure thought in your head."

"Well, I do think about cheese a lot," I started, confused on where this was going.

Gabriel burst out laughing and then tugged his shirt off leaving me breathless. "That's great, but now I want to know what kind of sounds I can pull out of you."

"Okay," I squeaked, my eyes boring into his bare chest. His hands went to the waist of his pants, and suddenly I was really into slacks. In particularly, slacks that were on the ground. Which was where I wanted Gabriel's to be.

In what felt like an eternity, Gabriel undressed completely, leaving me burning and wet with desire. He had barely touched me, and already I wanted to climb him like Everest and ride him like an award-winning steed. Oh, we'd make great babies together.

The thought popped into my head so unceremoniously that I almost lost my cool but then Gabriel's hands were pulling down my bra straps, and the random thought was gone. All I could focus on was his hands on my flesh, his mouth on my skin, each action causing my body to flush and dance.

By the time he got me out of my underwear, my panties were ruined. I'd never felt so turned on in my entire life. Everything about him made me hot. From the way he gently cupped my breasts to the way he gripped the back of my legs as he hoisted me into his arms, I couldn't get enough of him.

So much so that I was surprised when my back hit the cloud-like bed. I'd expected us to end up doing it against the wall. Another thing about Gabriel that had me in knots.

I gripped the back of his head, his mouth attacking my breasts as if they were something he'd found on the buffet. And if you'd seen this man eat, you'd know he savors his meals. Wholly. Fully. Making sure to savor every part of it to the fullest. I should know, he took the same kind of pleasure to my pussy not too long ago. The very thought of it had me getting impatient for more.

Pushing at his shoulders, I tried to subtly hint at where I wanted him. Gabriel glanced up from my chest and chuckled. Okay, maybe I wasn't that subtle, but it still got me what I wanted. His mouth slid across my stomach until he settled his shoulders between my thighs, spreading me open to his gaze.

I held my breath, the anticipation of his mouth on my swollen clit killing me by the second. When it didn't immediately come, I almost cried out in frustration. Instead, I kept my displeasure to myself as a light kiss was pressed to the inside of my thigh. And then another. And another. Each one came even closer to where I wanted him. Needed him. Then just as I prepared myself for the onslaught on my core, he bypassed it to give the other thigh the same treatment.

This time I couldn't hold back my aggravation and growled. Gabriel's laugh reverberated through my skin, making my insides clench deliciously. Thankfully, he didn't comment on it but continued his trek, moving up the inside of my thigh. His hot breath lingered on my throbbing core, and I arched up slightly as if I could make him close those final inches.

A single stroke of the tip of his tongue circled around my clit, and I cried out. My hands tore at the bed beneath me, that small moment sending fissures of pleasure through me. I didn't have time to calm down from the first touch before he tasted me again. At first, just moving in slow, soft circles before turning into long hard strokes.

My breathing came in heavy, each lap of his tongue more prominent than the last, and I knew I wasn't going to last much longer. Just as I began to come, Gabriel slipped a finger inside of me, pumping it while my insides spasmed wildly.

"Gabriel," I gasped out, my fingers digging into his hair, fighting to pull him closer and push him away. It was almost too good. When he withdrew, I found myself disappointed and relieved. As much as he gave good oral, I wanted to feel him inside of me before time ran out, which could be any minute.

I reached out and wrapped my hand around the length of his cock, familiarizing myself with it. I didn't like to compare the three of them, it didn't really seem fair, but they all were well proportioned. Nothing crooked or weird. I didn't know why I was surprised. They're angels. Even their cocks are perfect.

Gabriel let me take my time touching him, not rushing me to the next phase. I licked my lips and stared down at his length. Did he taste the same way as a human? Even with the time crunch pressing down on us, I couldn't let the question go unanswered.

With my other hand, I gave Gabriel a slight push on his abs, and he took the hint to turn over. Now, hovering over him, I grasped him more firmly in my hand, pumping it up and down. I cupped his balls and squeezed slightly, causing him to groan. Dipping my head down, I licked the head of his cock, letting the taste of him settle in my mouth.

Yep. Just like a human. What was I expecting? Some kind of divine cum? I laughed at myself internally. You know, cause laughing out loud earlier had been such a good idea. Doing it with his manhood in my hand and mouth probably not a good idea.

Pushing my thoughts to the side, I focused on giving Gabriel the same treatment he had given me. I lapped at his head a few more times, before taking him fully into my mouth. I forced my throat to relax as I moved my mouth over him taking him in deeply. As I reached the base, I squeezed his balls once more. A hand went into my hair, and I took that as an encouraging sign.

Bopping my head up and down, I alternated cupping him and swallowing. Each sound I pulled from Gabriel fueled my desire to see him fall apart. To taste him.

Unfortunately, Gabriel had other ideas. Before I knew what was happening, I had been jerked off his length and was flat on my back, Gabriel looming over me. His eyes bore into me, and a lust-filled grin covered his mouth. I only had a moment to see it before my eyes rolled up into the back of my head as Gabriel slid into me all at once.

Gasping, I grabbed hold of his biceps.

"Are you alright?" Gabriel asked, pausing mid-thrust.

I nodded with a forced grin. "Oh, yeah. Just caught me off guard is all." Man, he might not seem much bigger than the others, but those few centimeters sure made a difference.

A dull ache started inside of me as he moved again. Each thrust made my fingers tighten on his arms. With my recent orgasm still so prevalent in my lower regions, the feel of him rubbing against my insides was bordering on painful. Telling myself not to be such a weenie, I powered through the sensitivity, at least until his fingers found my clit once more, and then I was screaming. My toes curled under and my arms and legs wrapped around him as he pounded into me.

When my orgasm hit me this time, it felt like I'd been literally hit. Like someone had punched me right in the ovaries, and all I could do was beg for more. Gabriel ducked under my arms and lifted my legs up higher until they straddled his shoulders, his hips pistoning into me.

"Gabriel," I cried out, my head moving from side to side, "I don't know if I can come again." I'd never begged a man not to make me come before. It was unheard of. No woman - or man, for that matter - didn't want to come.

But my cries fell on deaf ears. Gabriel pushed

into me, his eyes boring into mine as his finger circled my clit. My breath hitched once more, and then I was spiraling. I was briefly aware of Gabriel tensing against me, a grunt coming from him before he collapsed beside me on the bed.

"Oh. My. God," I said when I finally got my breath back.

"Now is this my dad God or a lamentation on my skills as a lover?" Gabriel asked, laying back on his folded arms.

"Both." I giggled to myself. We lay together for a few moments, our breathing the only sound in the room.

"Hey," Gabriel said out of the blue. "You know what?"

"What?" I asked, still smiling like a loon.

"This bed does feel like a cloud."

10

I was in the middle of a delicious dream, one in which I had all three angels in my bed and not a stitch of clothing on. A dream I doubted I'd ever get to come to life but still a girl could have her fantasies.

Lucifer's lips trailed along the side of my neck, placing hot wet kisses. I laid my head back against his shoulder and arched my back as Michael cupped my breasts, his large hands the perfect size. Twisting the peaks until it bordered on pain, I gasped, my thighs clamping down to stop the ache between my thighs. Unfortunately, they landed against the side of Gabriel's head.

"Hey there, now," Gabriel said, reminding me of where he was. Before I could apologize he dipped his head back down and gave me another reason to moan.

"You really should eat something you know," my mother's voice suggested, making me pop my head up. Penny Mehr sat next to us on the bed with a plate of pizza in her hands. "You're going to get a low blood sugar if you don't carb up."

"Mom!" I cried out just as Gabriel lapped at me, making my words come out as more of a moan. "Get out, mom. Get out of my head!"

My mother opened her mouth and started to say something, but what came out was ringing.

"What?" I asked, trying to get the hands that suddenly seemed everywhere off of me. "I can't understand you."

When my brain began to realize that the ringing was happening outside of my head, the foursome disappeared, and I jerked awake. The incessant ringing of my phone greeted me. What the fuck? I opened my eyes and saw the pristine white ceiling above me and panicked. Where was I?

I sat up in bed and saw the rumpled sheets and the half-opened suitcase and remembered I was on a case. At a spa. Which I hadn't done anything on yet to make my stay worthwhile.

The scattered clothes from Gabriel the night before made me smile. Well, I couldn't say I had done nothing. Doing an angel was quite an achievement.

I suddenly remembered the other achievement that had been ruined by my mother's appearance. Man, I either had mommy issues or I just had one messed up brain. Shaking my dream off, I grabbed my phone off the nightstand, putting it to my ear and started to pick up Gabriel's clothes. "This is Jane."

"Jane!" Mandy yelled into my ear, and I leaned away from the sound. "I've been calling you all morning."

"Good morning to you, too," I grumbled, as I gathered yet another suit jacket to add to my growing collection. Really, these guys needed to start finding something to do with their clothes 'cause at this rate I was going to end up having enough for my own men's department store.

"Sorry, you're right. Good morning." Mandy sighed, and I could literally hear her tugging at her hair. "I'm just a bit stressed. This murder case is kicking our asses. We have one guy we are pretty sure is the killer, but we keep missing him."

I frowned. "I'm sorry. I hope O'Connor isn't

taking it out on you. There are two of you on the case. It's not like you're doing it on purpose."

"No, no." Mandy quickly said. "Nothing like that. The captain is breathing down our necks as well as the reporters, all wanting to know when we'll be getting the killer off the streets. Which was why I was calling you. Please tell me you solved the robberies already, so you can help us with this?"

Guilt ate at me. Here I was using up the city's time and resources to lounge around the beach, eat lots of food, and have crazy angel sex. Okay, the last bit I wouldn't feel guilty about because it was HAWT! I'd never been pushed so far in sex in my life, and I couldn't say that I hated it. In fact, if Gabriel hadn't lost his corporeal self and had to get back to work, I'd have begged him to rock my world again.

"I'm sorry, Mandy. I haven't found anything yet," I admitted, tensing as I waited for her to explode. Except it never came.

"Not surprised. That's the way my day is going." Mandy let out a depressing sigh, it was even worse than having her yell at me. Now I really felt bad.

"But don't worry," I added, holding Gabriel's clothes to me tightly. "I'm going to scour this place until I find the thief and then I will be there to help you. I promise."

Mandy sighed again even more dejected. "I'm sure you will. But please be careful. You might only be looking for a thief, but it could easily go badly. I wouldn't want to be looking for two killers."

"I'll be safe, I promise. No crazy antics for this gal." I smiled, hoping to get a laugh out of my best friend.

"Okay, I've got to go. I'll check in later." Mandy hung up without so much as a snicker.

Damn. That case must really be draining the life out of her. I suddenly wanted more than anything to catch this burglar and get to Mandy.

I bundled up Gabriel's clothes and set them to the side of my suitcase to deal with later. Digging through my bag, I searched for something acceptable to wear while sleuthing around the spa. Grabbing a tight, mint colored skirt and dark green top, I laid them out on the bed and then went to take a quick shower.

By the time I got out of the shower more than just my clothes were waiting for me on my bed. Michael sat on the edge, one leg crossed over the other, his eyes scanning the room.

"Hey," I greeted, very much aware that I had

left the bathroom naked and only had a small towel to dry my hair. Instead of freaking out, I decided to just go with it. He couldn't make me feel uncomfortable unless I let him. Besides, he'd already seen me naked, it's not like it was anything new.

"Hello," Michael greeted in return, his eyes scanning over my form. There was a certain heat there as well as appreciation, but he didn't try to start anything. Not like Lucifer would have. Instead, he simply watched me dry my hair.

"Were you here for a certain reason?" I asked, pulling my underwear up my legs. "Not that I mind your company."

Michael smiled one of his rare smiles that made me suddenly wish he would try something. "I enjoy your company as well." We exchanged a soft look for a moment before he cleared his throat and got serious. "But I did come here for a reason. I found out more about our little situation." He gestured between us, but I was at a loss.

"What situation?"

His words caught in his throat, his blue eyes watching me intently as I put on my bra. It seemed I wasn't the only one affected. Too bad I had thoughts of Mandy's depressed voice in my mind.

Shaking his head, Michael seemed to find his

bearings. "The situation regarding your blood and our sudden corporeal form."

"Oh. That." I tried to listen as intently as I could as I finished getting dressed. "What about it?"

Michael laced his fingers around his knee, pulling his crossed leg closer to him. "Well, it seems like we are able to take in some of your essence so to speak. Some of your humanity is passed to us which is what allows us to become solid."

"Okay," I drew out, not sure if this was a bad or good thing. "Are we happy or upset about this?"

"Curious would better describe it." Michael's eyes crinkled at the sides. "We don't know much more about it. Only the how, not the why. There are many questions unanswered in this regard, but I am unable to find answers. Even Father does not have anything to offer me. For all I know, it's part of His plan."

I snorted at that as I zipped up my skirt.

"You laugh, but He has used the same excuse on more than one occasion. Many times, it has proved to be a good thing. So, I will let it be for now."

I frowned, pulling my button-up shirt on. "How can that be? The all-mighty Archangel Michael is just going to go with the flow?" I raised a brow, and Michael suddenly stood from the bed.

Moving over to where I stood, his hands caught mine where I was buttoning my shirt, making them tingle pleasantly. "It's not that I don't care about what happens. It's more that I'm not sure I want to know."

"Why not?"

A small smile curled his lips. "Because that might mean I have to stop seeing you, and I'm not sure if I'm ready for that."

"Oh." My cheeks hurt from smiling so much. "Well, I'm happy you're not bothered by it, because I'm not ready to stop seeing you either." I stumbled over my words, my face red and my heart pounding like a drum.

"In fact," - Michael's fingers traced the line of my shirt, still unbuttoned and exposing my bra - "I was hoping to see a bit more of you."

I giggled nervously and then remembered Mandy and how stressed out she sounded. I moved away from Michael's finger before it could touch my bare skin, because we all knew my self-control was not that good.

"Don't you want to?" Michael arched a brow, his eyes on me.

Shaking my head, I gave him a weak smile. "No, it's not that. I'd *love* to show you more of me, but I am supposed to be here to catch a thief, and so far, I haven't done anything toward finding him or her. So as much as I want to, I can't." Even as I said it, my ovaries were crying out in dismay.

Michael's expression smoothed out and he inclined his head. "I understand. Your duties come before pleasure. I can admire that."

"You can?" I pressed my knuckles to the sides of my face, a bit apprehensive about turning him down.

"Yes, of course. I'm not some human that can't control himself." Michael snickered.

I threw myself at him in a stupid moment, which ended with me face first on the bed and a body full of tingles. Laughing at myself, I rolled over and stared up at Michael. "Well, I guess I'm done for the day, just let me crawl up in this bed and hide until my mortification passes."

"I'd offer you a hand up …" Michael trailed off, staring at his hand and then chuckled. "Well, we'd be back to square one."

"Yeah," I sighed and fell back on the bed. Staring up at the ceiling, I realized something. "You know, I have no idea where to start to look for this guy. Mandy said they thought it was an inside job, but there are so many employees here. It could be anyone."

Michael leaned over the bed so that I could see him. "Perhaps you should start by asking around." He turned his head and glanced around the room. "These rooms seem pretty well kept. I would think that it would be pretty hard for anyone to come in here and steal your valuables."

"Not unless you have a special key," I told him. "It's all electronic. Though, I suppose there are ways to copy them. Not that I expect anyone in Blessed Falls to be that computer savvy."

"Then you must ask around. Find out who has access to the rooms or to the device that makes those keys."

I sat up on the bed and stood. "That's a good idea actually. Need to get a list of potentials, then go from there. Thank you." I offered Michael a grateful smile. "I'd kiss you, but you know …"

Michael smirked. "I know."

Slipping on my heels, I finished buttoning my shirt and headed for the door. Before I got there, Michael called out to me.

"Yes?" I turned to look back at him.

Michael waited in the archway of the bedroom,

his eyes intently on me. "I wasn't just talking about sex, you know. I do want to see more of you. Outside of the bedroom."

My nose crinkled up. "You mean, like a date."

His lips tipped up at my words. "Yes, like a date. I would like to date you. All of us would."

"You've already talked about it with the others?" My mouth dropped open slightly. I didn't think they didn't talk about me amongst themselves. I mean, they're guys. Guys talk. But I didn't think they talked about that kind of stuff.

"Yes." Michael moved across the room, his gaze still focused on me. "Gabriel mentioned you took him to a buffet last night, and there was an interesting altercation with some females. He got the impression that you don't quite feel a hundred percent with us, and we wish to change that."

"You do?"

Michael nodded. "Yes, there's a reason we have lingered around you."

"Obviously." I rolled my eyes. "I can see you and others can't, and now the whole 'being able to touch you' thing."

Shaking his head, Michael chuckled. "No, it's not that at all. Okay, so partially it is. We were drawn to you before we knew you could see us.

Before we knew we could touch you. Taste you. Care for you." His eyes filled with an emotion I couldn't describe. "We don't want you to think that we are only around you because we have no other options."

"Aren't you though?" I asked, hating myself for being so insecure. "I'm not really that remarkable, despite everything else."

"You're wrong," Michael told me, his voice low and hypnotizing. "You're the most remarkable human I've ever met. And I've met my fair share."

Licking my lips, I breathed, "That's good to know."

"And now you do." Michael leaned forward, his lips brushing mine. When I opened my eyes, Michael was gone, and my lips buzzed in his wake.

11

With my lips still buzzing from Michael's kiss, I started toward the lobby. If there was anywhere to start asking questions, that'd be it.

I hung around in the lobby, watching people check in to the resort and some checking out. The manager came out a few times and gave me the evil eyes, before heading to a door marked 'Private.'

Know how I said the lobby was the best place to ask questions? I'd been wrong. So totally wrong. Who hung out in the lobby? Nobody, that's who. Everyone was either enjoying the spa or working in the employee only areas.

One of those things I wasn't supposed to do, but the other … I eyeballed a woman coming out of one of the employee only rooms. From the peek I got in as she exited, it looked like some kind of changing room. Maybe I could get some real answers if I pretended to be one of them? Maybe being a guest wasn't the answer, but being an employee was!

Suddenly excited about my new plan, my eyes darted around as I hustled over to the door. I slipped inside and let out a breath. Empty. Great.

My eyes took in the lockers lining the wall and relaxed. Just what I needed. Now, I needed to find someone's uniform I could borrow. I tried a bunch of the lockers, but most of them were locked. I finally found one that hadn't been shut all the way and did a little happy dance.

"What are you doing?" Lucifer asked, making me jump and spin around.

I glanced around the room quickly before pointing a finger at Lucifer. "Don't do that! I'm in a very precarious position. If anyone catches me, my cover will be blown. Mandy will be devastated, and I'll have no more money coming in from the PD."

Lucifer held his hands up in front of him. "My apologies. I was not aware you were preoccupied."

"Well, I am. Now shush. I'm trying to steal stuff." I turned away from him and to the open locker. I pulled out a white and blue uniform, the same kind as the cleaning ladies. Score.

I started to take my clothes off to put the new ones on when Lucifer said, "I'm not an expert on women's clothing, but I don't believe that is your size."

Frowning, I glanced down at the tag. Extra-Large. It would drown me, but I didn't really have many options. It'd have to do.

"I'll make do," I told him as I shimmied into the dress. Zipping it up, it hung around me like a circus tent. Well, crap. This wasn't going to work.

Looking up from my predicament, I saw Lucifer holding his hand in a fist against his mouth, obviously trying not to laugh. "Stop laughing. It's not that funny."

"It is actually."

"No," I snapped. "It's not."

I growled and slapped at the uniform. For once in my life, I wished for larger hips. Since no one was granting wishes today, I searched around for something to tie around my waist. Digging back into 'Marty's' locker, I almost cried out when I found an apron bundled at the bottom of the locker.

Quickly wrapping it around my waist, I tied it tight, having to wrap the ties around me twice to shorten the string. Looking over myself in the locker room mirror, I frowned. Still not great but better. My eyes caught a white-ish stain near the bottom, and I grimaced. Don't think about it. It's just mayo. Just mayo.

"How do I look?" I asked Lucifer. "Like a maid, right?"

Lucifer shrugged a shoulder. "I suppose, but I thought you were supposed to wear high heels and those thigh high stockings. You know, with the feather duster." He grinned, tucking his hands into his pockets.

Snorting, I moved past him. "Of course, you'd think of the porno version. I forgot who I was talking to." I pushed out of the locker room and headed toward where I saw the other women go, Lucifer hot on my heels which I hadn't changed out of. Hopefully, nobody noticed them. I didn't see many real-life maids wearing high heels. I could imagine the blisters already.

The room was dimly lit with a few caged areas. Rows of shelves were stacked with cleaning products and those little toiletries they put in your room. I glanced around and grabbed a handful shoving them into my apron pocket.

"Real smooth."

I shot a glare at Lucifer but didn't reply. Voices were coming from deeper in the room. It sounded like they were having a meeting of some sort.

"Hey, you new?" a brunette woman smoking a cigarette asked as she came up beside me.

Hiding my shaking hands, I nodded. "Yes, just started. I hate to admit it, but I'm kind of lost. They told me to come in here to get set up, but I lost my shadow."

"Oh, yeah." The woman nodded as if she knew exactly what I was talking about. "Just keep going. Their handing out assignments now so you're just in time."

"Oh great," I answered, clasping my hands in front of me. I lingered for a second and then started toward the talking.

"I'm Abigail by the way." The smoking women held out her hand to me, and I shook it quickly. "But you can call me Abby. Everyone does, whether I like it or not."

"Uh, okay, Abigail." I cleared my throat and shot a look at Lucifer who seemed way too amused by the whole situation. "I'm Patty."

Abigail snorted. "Of course, you are."

We finally arrived at the back of a group of about two dozen women all dressed like Abigail and me. An older woman in a suit stood at the front of the group with a clipboard barking out orders.

"That's Crystal, the housekeeping manager," Abigail whispered to me. "She's a real bitch."

I nodded stiffly and tried to make myself as inconspicuous as possible but failed when Crystal caught sight of me.

Pointing a finger at me, she shouted, "You!"

"Me?" I glanced around as if there was someone else behind me.

"Yeah, you. Who are you?"

I blanched and then cleared my throat. "I'm Patty."

Crystal looked down at her clipboard and then back to me, shaking her head. "I don't have a Patty. What are you doing here?"

My hands started to sweat as panic set in. My eyes darted around the room, all the other maids were staring straight at me. "I'm … I'm new. Just started today."

"No, you didn't. I haven't hired any new people," Crystal snapped back as if daring me to prove me wrong. I so wished I could slink out the back, but I couldn't. I had to just go with it.

"You didn't. Riley, I mean, Mr. Parks did." I

faked a blush, hoping they thought maybe I was a piece of eye candy Riley hired behind her back.

There was a hushed silence for a moment before all their eyes turned to Crystal, whose face had turned to hard stone. If she had super powers, I was sure in that moment she would have shot a death laser through my chest.

Thankfully, all she did was cluck her tongue and growl. "Of course, he did, the spineless cunt." She let out a heavy breath before pointing toward another one, this one with dark red hair piled on top of her head, a chipper smile on her face. "Okay, Patty, you're with Rose. She'll show you the ropes."

"Okay," I answered, letting out a breath. Lucky. Lucky. That could have gone so wrong for me.

Lucifer seemed to think so as well. "I smell something foul in here, and it's not just the stain on your apron." I discreetly flipped him off which only made him grin. "That Crystal woman seems a bit off."

"You think," I said without thinking, causing Abigail to look at me strangely. I quickly added, "Rose will be a good trainer?"

Abigail lifted a shoulder. "She's as good as any. Not much up here though." She pointed a long-painted nail at her forehead.

"Uh huh," I mused before turning back to Crystal and her announcements. She went on a bit longer than I expected. I started to zone out, and then before I realized how much time had passed, Rose came bounding toward me with way too much energy in her step.

"Hi! I'm Rose. You must be Patty. I'm so excited to be your trainer. I love being a maid. Do you love being a maid? I think it's got to be one of the best jobs in the world, don't you?" She finally stopped to let me answer, her big hazel eyes blinking at me expectantly.

I glanced over at Abigail who rolled her eyes. Forcing a smile, I said, "Yeah. It's pretty great. Hey, not to be a gossip, but what can you tell me about—"

"No time for talking!" Rose announced, her finger in the air like some kind of robot. "We have to get going, or we'll get behind. Can't have any of our guests sitting on a dirty toilet, now can we?" she asked me with a smile and a slight tilt of her head.

Could you say creepy? It was like she was some kind of Stepford wife or something. No one should be that excited about cleaning toilets. It was just unnatural.

I gave Abigail a helpless look, but she just

chuckled and patted me on the shoulder. "Good luck."

Rose grabbed my arm and dragged me over to where the carts were lined up. "You want to fill your cart every morning. Make sure you get enough supplies because having to come back will dock time off your schedule and put you behind."

"We wouldn't want that," I muttered, but Rose caught it.

"Exactly!" The screeching end of her voice made me wince, and I knew I was going to need some pain medicine before the end of the day.

"So, we fill our carts for exactly what we need plus a little extra." Her eyes darted to the side for a moment before leaning toward me. "There have been some guests with sticky fingers."

This had my ears perking up. "Sticky fingers?"

"Shh!" Rose put her finger to her mouth, her eyes going wide. "We can't talk about it, or Crystal will get upset. The manager already got onto her about missing inventory, so you must be diligent in making sure no one takes from your cart. Never leave it alone. Got it?" Her eyes were serious, the most serious I'd seen her so far.

I nodded my head numbly, my mind focused on what she had told me so far. So, guests were stealing toiletries and stuff like that. I thought about the mini shampoos in my pocket. Not surprising. Everyone did it. That and the robes. I knew I'd be taking mine with me the moment I left. Besides, it'd be charged to the city in any case.

Thankfully, Lucifer didn't follow me on my first day of training. I had a hard enough time fitting in without his commentary to add to it. Rose talked enough for the lot of us as it was.

I followed Rose around for a while going from one room to another and thought about what I'd learned. The maids clearly feared Crystal. They didn't want to upset her about more thefts. It made me wonder what other ones had occurred that the managers didn't know about.

"Hey, Rose," I asked as I cleaned the mirror in one of the bathrooms, "do people steal a lot here? Like more than just toiletries?"

Rose stood from where she was cleaning a toilet, something she had deemed me not ready to do yet. Thank God. "Um, I guess. Little things disappear all the time. Either stolen or misplaced."

"Like what?" I asked, and the suspicious look she gave me made me add, "I just want to know if I should keep my purse in my car is all."

Her eyes widened. "Oh, no, nothing like that.

It's mostly, like, guests' belongings and such. Sometimes stationery but nothing big." She paused and then said, "Actually, there was this one incident a few weeks ago." She moved past me and peeked out the bathroom door before coming back in and shutting it. "A guest had put some jewelry in the room safe. Some really expensive stuff. Nothing I could afford for sure," Rose rambled on. "But anyway, it came up stolen!"

"No!" I gasped, putting my hand on my chest. "What happened?"

Rose shrugged. "No one knows. The police were involved and everything."

"Did they ever catch them? The thief I mean."

Rose shook her head sadly. "Not as far as I know, but they haven't said anything else about it. So, we all assumed it was taken care of."

"So, is that why Crystal is all upset with Mr. Parks?" I asked, trying not to prod too much.

Laughter billowed out of Rose. "Oh no. Well, I mean, yeah, they fought about it. Mr. Parks said it was one of us girls but none of us could have broken into that safe. Not without help." She shook her head and then cleared her throat. "But anyway, that's not why she doesn't like Mr. Parks."

"It's not?"

"No," she waved her toilet brush in the air, and I stepped back from her just in case of sprayage. "It's because he cheated on her."

"Really?" I gaped from real shock. The fact that anyone would want to date Riley was shocking enough, but two women did? Unbelievable.

"Yep. With one of her own cleaning girls." Rose pressed her lips together in a grim line. "Well, anyway, she's dating the security guy now. Has been for almost a year, but still, it's obvious she hasn't gotten over it. Though I think Ernie is way better for her anyway."

"Obviously." I noted that. Ernie, the security guy. Definitely someone to look into.

"If I were you, I'd steer clear of Mr. Parks and stay on Crystal's good side unless you want to be out of a job." She pointed the toilet brush at me and then went back to cleaning the toilet.

"I'll keep that in mind," I said, turning back to the mirror. So, Riley and Crystal fought over the thefts. Crystal was dating the security guy. Something stunk and not just this person's toilet bowl.

12

The next morning, I sat at my table eating the fluffiest scrambled eggs I'd ever put in my mouth. It was as if someone took one look at the beds at this place and thought, "You know what would taste good? Cloud eggs." And then they just did it. I didn't even need to put my usual hot sauce on them like I usually did. They were that good.

I was so engrossed by my eggs that I didn't see Michael join me until he spoke.

"I cannot figure out if I should be jealous or not?"

"Oh, be jealous." I smirked with a mouth full of eggs. Not the sexiest look but my mouth felt like a million bucks. I could give up being sexy for one morning.

Michael made a disbelieving sound, and I glanced up from my eggs. He stood beside me looking as delicious as the eggs on my plate. His blonde hair looked like he had been running his hand through it. His chiseled jaw was even more defined this morning, the muscle there tensed until I thought it might break.

"What's your problem?" I scooped up another fork full of eggs and shoveled it into my mouth. "Why the sour puss?"

"I am not a sour puss," Michael snapped, his biceps flexing as he crossed them over his chest.

I sighed and dropped my fork onto my plate and picked up my knife. Lucky for me there wasn't anyone else in the breakfast area. I'd been late getting up after my one and only day of being a maid, something I will never repeat again. My feet just couldn't take it. Plus, people were disgusting. Maids did not get paid enough to deal with the monstrosity of the things we had to deal with yesterday.

One room in particular would forever be ingrained in my mind. I couldn't even think about it let alone tell anyone. Let's just say it involved way too many used condoms and sheets that would be better off burned than cleaned.

The sting of the knife cut through my dirty thoughts as I pressed the knife to my forearm. I'd been abusing my fingers way too much lately and not in a good way. I could deal with a tiny cut on my arm. I could blame it on clumsiness or maybe even work-related. I wondered if I could claim workman comp for this?

"What are you doing?" Michael asked, his eyes fixed on the blood coming from the small cut.

"Fixing your face. Now, drink up." I held my arm up to him. Michael looked at it suspiciously as if I had poisoned it somehow. Really, what was up his butt? Someone obviously needed to get laid. "Come on, hurry up. This is a fancy place. They won't leave me alone for very long. If their noses were shoved any further up my ass, they'd be eating my breakfast for me."

Quirking a brow, Michael leaned forward and pressed his mouth to my arm. The reaction was immediate, and I withdrew my arm, pressing my napkin to it. It wasn't a deep cut, it'd stop bleeding easily. I wasn't suicidal. I might want angelic cock but not enough to kill myself for it.

Michael took the seat across from me and used

the napkin on his side to wipe the blood from his mouth. "Thank you, but I don't see how this will improve my mood."

Forcing myself not to sigh at his drama queen attitude, I met the eyes of a waiter who had just come in to handle their one customer like he had five minutes before. See, nose in ass. I raised my hand up, gesturing for him - Tim - to come over. He practically skipped toward me like a dog eager to see his owner.

"What can I do for you, beautiful?" He grinned so big I could see his molars, his hands rubbing together in front of him. Was he rubbing lotion on? Or had he just finished practicing for his evil dark lord speech? You know the one. Where they give away their big plan right before they think they are going to kill you, but then you end up getting away and saving the day because they had literally told you their plan. Stupid, really.

Not saying any of the thoughts running through my head, I picked my fork up and pointed it at Michael. "Could I get a plate of these heavenly eggs?"

Michael snorted at my description which I answered with a wink.

"And isn't this a yummy piece of sunrise." Tim

gaped at Michael for a moment, one hand to his chest. Okay, he wasn't a brown-noser. He just didn't care for what I had between my thighs. I could respect that. If my only customer were taking their sweet ass time eating while I could be in the back gossiping with the rest of the crew, I'd be - okay, I wouldn't even be close to as nice as this guy - I'd be a dick. Just so they would leave as quickly as possible. The fact Tim had even bothered to check on me was a testament to his character. Or his need for me to get the fuck out. Though, I had a feeling that now that Michael was here, his tune had changed.

"This is Michael." I pointed with my fork. "And he is having a bad day." I poked my lip out in a pout and gave Michael my best puppy dog eyes.

"I am not having a bad day," Michael growled, his eyes searing into me. I cocked a brow and looked up at Tim and then back to Michael. Tapping his silverware against the table, Michael sighed. "Fine. You win. Bring me the eggs."

"See?" I lifted a forkful to my mouth. "Food solves everything."

"Preach it." Tim pursed his lips, waved a finger. "I'll be right back with your eggs."

I nodded, and Tim started walking away. Before

he could get very far, I had a wicked idea. "Hold up, Tim! Can you bring me some hot sauce?"

Tim waved a hand back letting me know he heard me before disappearing behind the double doors to the kitchen.

"Soooo …" I drew out, picking up the glass of orange juice that had been squeezed by angels. The fat babies in diaper kind, not the hunk-a-hunk of burning love type. Though, I wasn't so sure I wouldn't drink something Michael hand squeezed for me. Especially, if it involved him naked in the kitchen, a tiny apron the only thing covering his Johnson. Okay, sidetracked. I really needed to get my mind out of the gutter. I blame the angels. I was only human, and they were too beautiful and charming to not want to have all to myself all the time.

"So?" Michael answered back, not budging at all.

"Are you really going to make me ask again?" I sat my drink down and leaned back in my seat, my hands settled on my stomach. "Because I can do this all day. Just ask Mandy. There's never been a time that I wasn't able to get the truth from her."

"I'm an angel, an archangel at that. I doubt you

can make me do anything I don't want to do." The superior tone in his voice made me laugh.

"You don't think I can?" my lips curved up into a cheeky grin. "If I could get Becka Adams, who is quite the tight-lipped little Nancy, to spill all her dirty secrets, then I think I can get one angel to tell me why he's acting like the Devil took his favorite toy."

Michael flinched.

My eyes widened a fraction, and I leaned my elbow on my chair, my hand covering my mouth as I tried and failed to stifle my laughter. "You're serious. You're really, really serious. Wow. I didn't expect this. I mean, I thought you were all on board with the whole 'let's all get naked and sweaty with Jane' thing." When Michael didn't answer and, if possible, got even more broody, I clammed up, suddenly feeling bad about laughing. "Should I apologize?"

"For what?" Michael asked.

I started to answer and then stopped when Tim came sauntering back out with Michael's plate of eggs. He sat the bottle of hot sauce on the table as well and smiled. "Is there anything else I can get you?"

"No, we're good." I smiled up at him.

Tim nodded and started to leave but then stopped and turned back to us. "Let me know if the eggs don't do it. Some of us employees are having a party tonight right here in the breakfast hall. A real 'leave your keys at home' kind. If it doesn't turn his day right side up, then nothing will."

His eyes moved up and down Michael as if he were savoring him. I understood. I'd been there before. I still got a bit breathless with each meeting. Tim offered us a coy grin and a wink before leaving.

A party, huh? Might be fun. God knew we needed some. And based on the sour expression on Michael's face, he definitely needed some. But first I had to fix what was broken.

"Are you mad that I had sex with Lucifer and Gabriel?" I asked, deciding to rip the band-aid off in one swift go.

"No, no." Michael shook his head, fiddling with his fork before taking a tentative bite of his eggs. I watched, only partially interested in his reaction to the first human food he'd ever eaten. And I wasn't disappointed.

His eyes closed for a moment, his jaw moving up and down as he took his time rolling it around in his mouth. He seemed to be trying to get as much flavor out of it as possible before he finally swallowed. His eyes opened.

"Good?" I asked, leaning forward, a bit eager to learn what he thought.

Michael didn't answer but took another bite, this time much larger than the last. After a few seconds, it was like he had forgotten what we were talking about and only had eyes for the food on his plate. Not that I was upset. That had been the whole point, but I had a feeling it was only putting off the inevitable.

"I am not upset that you had intercourse with Lucifer and Gabriel," Michael admitted when his plate was half empty.

"You're not?"

"No."

When he didn't say anything else on the matter, I had to push my luck. "Okay, so if you're not upset about the sex, then what is it?"

Michael sat his fork down and clasped his hands in front of him, his face closing down. "There was an argument between the three of us."

"An argument?" I scooched forward in my seat, my face pinched with concern. I'd seen them fight before. It wasn't a pretty picture. The world itself shook, and feelings were hurt. If you'd ever had to cheer up the literal Devil, you wouldn't want to hear them fighting either.

"Yes, it was implied that … well … that you enjoyed your time with them more than you did with me." His eyes dipped down, and I could have cried. I didn't because it would have made the whole thing worse, but I did push my chair back and move over to his side.

Pulling his chair out, I leaned down and placed my hands on either side of his face. I took his mouth with mine, pouring as much feeling into it as I possibly could. Of all of them, I never expected Michael to the be the insecure one. Lucifer, sure. He was a big baby about most things. God forbid he wasn't the center of attention. But not strong, confident Michael. The hand of God.

I released his mouth with a squelching sound. He stared up at me with hooded eyes and a satisfied grin on his lips. Happy to have gotten the reaction I'd hoped for, I went back to my seat.

"Now, are we good?" I asked, before finishing off my eggs.

Michael cleared his throat and moved his chair back up to the table. Instead of answering me, he picked up the bottle of hot sauce. "Do you put this on your food?"

"Yes."

One brow lifted, and Michael opened the top and poured a substantial amount onto the remaining eggs on his plate. I made a small, strangled noise in the back of my throat, but held it back, letting him cover his plate with it. My fingers dug into the table as I watched him fill his fork with it and, in slow motion, lift it to his mouth.

I should have told him what to expect. I'd done so with Gabriel. Well, kind of but I couldn't help myself. The very fact that he hadn't asked and had just dumped a shit-ton on his food was reason enough to let him learn his lesson the hard way.

Michael's reaction was immediate. His eyes bulged from his head, and he tried to spit the taste out but only succeeded making himself look like a dribbling weirdo. I lifted my cup of orange juice up and handed it to him. He yanked it from my hands, spilling some over onto my hands.

While he drained the cup, I wiped my hands off on my napkin and smiled. "So, this party?"

13

"I said I was sorry," I exclaimed for the millionth time since breakfast.

"I didn't say anything." Michael stared forward, not looking at me as we made our way toward the party Tim had invited us to.

"You don't have to, I can see it in your face. You're still pissed." I huffed and crossed my arms over my sparkly halter top. I didn't know what kind of party it was, but the way Tim had made it sound mean, it was more booze and wine coolers than caviar and scotch, which worked for me. I'd always been a cheap drunk. My five-dollar bottles of wine at home could attest to that.

"I apologize if my face has given you that impression." Michael tucked his hands into his pockets, his eyes still facing forward. He had lost his corporeal form a bit after breakfast, and before that he had been reaming into me about warning a friend. Really, if I'd known he was going to be such a big baby about it, I wouldn't have let him try it at all.

He'd disappeared after that, to do God knew what. Probably to pout. Freaking baby. Then he popped up just five minutes before I planned to leave for Tim's party, looking way better than he should. I mean, Michael always looked good, but tonight, he looked particularly biteable.

He must have gotten some pointers from the others or found some old T.V. show to watch because he wouldn't have picked what he was wearing on his own. Tight, butt-hugging black pants and a button-down, short-sleeved shirt. I didn't see Michael in button downs often. Usually, his go-to attire was sweaters and thick V-necks, a 'casual manager' kind of a look.

I didn't need any persuasion to give him a bit of the red stuff to make him material again.

I grabbed his arm and stopped him before we could get any further. "Look, can we just put the whole hot sauce thing behind us? You're the one who wanted to go on a date with me. This party tonight can be that."

"Really?" Michael's brow furrowed. "A party counts? I thought we had to be alone for it to be a date."

"No, no." I shook my head, waving a hand in front of me. "A date can be anything. Even sitting in the room watching T.V. and binging out. Though most of the time that just ends up with people getting naked and sweaty." I giggled, but it died off at the heated look in Michael's eyes.

Michael picked up my hand and brought it up to his lips, brushing his mouth against it. "Then I would be happy to escort you."

A bit breathless, I said, "Okay." The distance between us seemed to close, and I could feel my eyelids getting heavy as I pushed up on my tiptoes. We were just moments from pressing our lips together when a gaggle of giggling women all dolled up like us came barreling through the hallway.

Breaking apart but without lessening the tension between us, I grabbed Michael's hand and led him toward the direction the women had gone. There was only one place they could be heading, and if the pounding of the bass reverberating beneath my feet was anything to go by, we were going in the right direction.

We pushed open the door to the breakfast hall and were immediately assaulted by the loud music. How the rest of the spa couldn't hear it was beyond me. I hadn't heard a single thing from my room. I'd never have known there was a wild party going on over here had Tim not invited me.

I hadn't gotten more than a few steps into the hall before Rose found me. Her red hair was pinned up in an elaborate do and wore a flowery sundress. Not something I'd have picked for this kind of party but pretty all the same.

"Patty!" she cried out, grabbing my hands. "We all thought you quit when you didn't show up to work today."

"Oh, uh." I glanced up at Michael and then back to Rose. "I kind of did."

"Oh, poo. And after you were getting so good too." Rose pouted, and then a second later she was back, beaming like a lighthouse. "Hi, I'm Rose." She held her hand out to Michael and blushed as he took it into his own. A real charmer that one and he didn't have to say a word.

"This is my boyfriend, Michael," I said auto-matically and then clamped my hand over my mouth, my eyes shooting to the archangel. He arched a brow but didn't correct me.

Rose thankfully didn't notice the exchange. "Well, it's nice to meet you. And have fun. I hope we get to see each other more. Even though you won't be my trainee anymore."

"You too," I muttered and watched her flounce away before turning to Michael. "I hope that was okay, calling you my boyfriend like that."

"I didn't mind. Though I hardly constitute as a boy." He eyed me in a way that had my panties drenched in seconds.

"Of course not. It's just an expression. A way to say we're together."

"And are we?"

"Together?" I wrung my hands in front of me. "Well, I'd hope so. I don't exactly show my goodies to just anyone, Lucifer and Gabriel aside."

"And are they your boyfriends as well?" Michael wrapped an arm around my waist leading me further into the room. The beat of the music pulsed through my veins along with my pounding heart. How exactly did I answer this? I mean, we hadn't really had a big group discussion about what we were. I'd hate to presume, but I had a feeling Gabriel and Lucifer would be okay with me calling them my boyfriends.

"Yeah." I grinned up at him finally, stopping myself from fretting over it anymore. "You all are. Is that okay?" I peeked up at him looking for his reaction.

"If it makes you happy, I do not have a problem with it." Michael drew me up against him, so that our bodies lined up, his hand taking mine in his. "Now, show me how to dance like a human would."

Giggling despite myself, I wrapped my other arm around Michael's neck and moved my body to the beat. My hips pressed against his, urging him to move with me. We swayed and moved to the beat, getting lost in our movements and each other. Michael was a great dancer for someone who'd never danced to human music. I was sure the music in heaven was all harps and trumpets; hard to really dance to that. At least, not like this.

"Do all humans dance this way?" Michael asked after a moment, his body pressed so tightly against me that it was hard to tell where he ended and I began.

I shrugged. "Some don't. Like, if I didn't know you very well, I wouldn't do this." I turned around so that my back was to his front, my arms going over my head to latch onto his hair as I ground my ass into him. Michael's hands found my hips and matched my every movement with his own.

His face dipped down by my ears, his voice tickling the side of my neck. "So, since I am your boyfriend, it is alright to rub our bodies against each other in front of others? Should we have sex as well?"

His words made me shake my head laughing. "No, I mean, yes. We can, and I hope we will, but not right here." I turned back around, lacing my fingers in the hair at the base of his neck. "I just meant that we can dance however we wish, and most won't say anything. Or care if I know you or if I'd just met you."

"That's all very confusing." Michael held me closer, the skin between his eyes bunching together.

Smiling broadly, I stroked my finger between his eyes, soothing his confusion. "It can be. Humans are fickle. You should know that. What might be okay right now might be forbidden in an hour." I lifted a shoulder. "But I'm more of a live-in-the-moment kind of girl in any case. And at this moment, I want something to drink. I'm dying here." I released him and started toward the bar area they had set up.

Tim was there chatting up a rather well-muscled fellow. When he saw us approach, his eyes lit up. "I see you found your way here. How's the sourpuss doing?"

"The sourpuss is fine. Thank you for asking," Michael answered before I could. "Jane would like a drink." He said it like there would be no more discussion, and I had to hold back my laughter.

"Oh-kay," Tim drew out, meeting my eyes. I shook my head and grinned. "Well, come on over here, my Viking king. Let me show you what I've got."

I stood at the bar, tapping my fingers on the top and swaying to the music. The person beside me living in a cloud of smoke turned around and bumped into me. "Uh, excuse you," I snapped. When I saw who it was all the blood drained from my face. "Uh. Abby. I mean, Abigail. How are you?"

"Fine. No thanks to your no-show." Abigail took a long drag of her cigarette and blew it in my direction. I coughed and waved a hand in front of my face. "I thought your name was Patty?"

"Uh, it is. Or was." I fumbled with my words. "I'm playing around with new names. Patty just seems so 1950s you know?"

"And Jane isn't?" Abigail snorted. "Well, whatever your name is. You really screwed us over today when Crystal was handing out assignments. I got stuck with your rooms as well as my own."

"I'm really sorry, Abigail." I winced, feeling bad she had to work twice as much because of me. "Cleaning just isn't for me."

"I got that impression from Rose." Abigail gestured her cigarette toward the redhead. "She won't say a negative thing toward anyone, but after a few years of working together, it's easy to decipher her language. You clean as well as a blind, deaf leper with a case of the chicken pox."

I grimaced. I hadn't really tried that hard. It was a fake job after all. I already had a job. One I was supposed to be doing now.

"Sorry about that," I apologized once more and then decided to try my luck. "Hey, I heard from …" I glanced at Rose and then changed what I was about to say. "… around that Crystal and the security manager are dating."

"If you could call it dating." Abigail made a disgusted noise. "It's more like he bums money off Crystal at any chance he can get, and she falls for his 'I'm so sad and pathetic, my mother's in the hospital' bit every time."

"You don't think his mother is really sick?" I asked, my eyes searching the crowd for Crystal and hopefully the mystery guy.

"Oh, I know she is, but that ain't why the dick wad needs the money."

"It's not?"

Abigail shook her head, putting her cigarette out in the ashtray as she blew out the last of the smoke. This time, thankfully, not in my direction. "Nope. That putz is in debt up to his eyeballs. Credit cards. Gambling. You name it."

"Here." Michael came up behind me and offered me a glass of some colorful mixture.

"Thanks." I smiled up at him and then gestured to Abigail. "Michael, this is Abigail."

"Abby," she corrected, a genuine smile on her lips. The first one I'd ever seen on her in the short time I'd known her. "Where did you find this one?"

"Oh, you know. Just lying around." I waved my hand in the air.

"Well, if I had a man like this waiting for me at home, I wouldn't be spending my days cleaning either. How do you even get out of bed in the morning?" Abigail smirked, her jokes all for fun and not at all leering at Michael like some had.

"It's a challenge but one I'm happy to have." I

took Michael's hand in my own, squeezing it before turning back to Abigail. "So, you were saying about the security manager? What's his name?"

"Ernie Slousky." Abigail pulled another cigarette out and lit the end, taking a long drag. "Why do you care so much?"

"Oh, uh. I'm just curious is all. I hope to get a different job here at the spa. Maybe in the kitchen or as a waitress." I hurried to make an excuse. I hated lying to her. Abigail seemed like a great friend if an unorthodox one.

"This Ernie fellow," Michael started, his front pressing up against my back. "You were lovers, yes?"

"Well, aren't you the perceptive one?" Abigail chuckled, her eyes alight with humor. "Yeah, Ernie and I shacked up a few times. Nothing permanent because I caught him stealing from my purse one time too many. Nobody steals from me and gets away with it." Abigail gave me a warning look as if I might try to take the cigarette right out of her hand.

"Gotcha." I tipped my glass to her with a smile. "Well, we're going to go dance some more. Enjoy the party."

"Oh, I will." Abigail turned back to the bar

where her glass sat and drained it in one gulp. Someone was going to get smashed.

"So, what now?" Michael asked as we made our way through the crowd.

I dug through my clutch and pulled out my phone. "Now, we pause our date, and I call Mandy."

14

Mandy asked me to come down to the station to talk about what I'd found out. I asked her why she couldn't get off her sweet ass and come to me, but she couldn't. Something about not being able to get away from their murder case without the feds jumping in on them.

"Are you sure you're okay with this?" I asked, pulling into the Blessed Falls Police Department parking lot. "I mean, this was supposed to be our date night, and I'm interrupting it with work."

Michael looked over at me from his side of the car. "Your work is important to you. I understand better than anyone how sometimes it has to come first."

The tone of his voice spoke volumes. It must be hard to be the hand of God. I couldn't imagine the pressure he probably had to deal with. If I thought God would care or even listen, I'd tell Him to ease up off Michael a bit. But as Michael said, our jobs are important. Not more important than each other but important enough that I wouldn't want to put my nose in his.

"Okay, but you don't have to come in. I can handle this really quick and then we can go back to the party or even go somewhere else." I squeezed his hand in mine. "Anywhere you want."

Bringing my hand up to his mouth, Michael kissed it. "I want to be where you are. The place doesn't matter."

My heart fluttered in my chest. This guy, seriously. If he was any sweeter, he'd be on one of those sappy channels my mother watched endlessly around Christmas time. Really, not all guys are that nice. Just ask my ex-boyfriends. I'm a bitch.

"Fine, but we're only going in for a minute to give her the update and then we are out of here." I grinned at him, before getting out of the car and heading inside.

Thankfully, it was late enough that Smith wasn't manning the front desk. A younger peppier version of her sat in Smith's seat and was more than happy to let us into the back without buzzing for Mandy.

I held Michael's hand and led him through the maze of desks. More than one set of eyes followed us from police officers and criminals alike. It seemed Michael had that kind of effect on people.

Searching the back, I tried to find Mandy's blonde head but came up blank. Thankfully, Officer Cutie – who I now knew as Tie - had set up shop at one of the desks and I hurried over to him.

"Hey, Tie, I'm—"

"Jane. Yeah, I remember. You helped with the Granes case a few weeks ago. Are you looking for Stevenson?" He pushed his glasses up his nose, his eyes darting back to his computer screen. "She's in conference room one with O'Connor."

"Thanks!" I started that way, but Tie stopped me.

"I'm warning you. They've been in there for hours with no progress. Tempers are high. So, if you're going in there, you better have good news." His eyes moved to Michael and then back to me, his shoulders hunching slightly. "You know, how O'Connor is."

"Understood." I patted him on the shoulder and then gestured for Michael to follow me.

Darting through the rest of the desks, I found the conference room they had set up shop in. Through the windows I could see O'Connor sitting at the table, his face buried in a file, his hair disheveled and his eyes tired. Mandy was nowhere in sight, and I considered waiting for her before going in, but then O'Connor looked up and saw me. Too late now.

Pushing the door open, I moved into the room with Michael on my tail. "Hey O'Connor, how's it going?"

"What do you want?" his question had no bite to it, making me worry the case they were working on was really getting to them. His weary eyes moved to Michael's large form, he frowned. "You can't just bring whoever you want back here. This is an ongoing investigation you know."

Michael didn't seem at all intimidated by O'Connor. Which he shouldn't. He was a bad ass angel and O'Connor was just a forty-year-old divorced man who used way too much hair product. Still, I had to play nice or Mandy would be up my ass about it.

"I know, I know." I held my hands up. The urge to tease him was nonexistent for once. All business.

"I just came by to tell you about a break in the burglary case."

"Oh?" his brows lifted and the tension in his form dropped a bit. When I didn't immediately start spouting off details, he gestured vigorously. "Don't make me wait all day, what is it?"

I hesitated. "Shouldn't we wait for Mandy to come back? I'd hate to repeat myself. Where is she by the way?" I glanced around the room covered in file boxes and papers, images tacked to a board like the one they'd used to brief me on the resort case, but no Mandy.

"She's on a coffee run."

"I didn't see her by the pot," I countered, not quite believing his story. Why would she tell me to come down if she wasn't even here? Freaking sneaky bitch.

O'Connor scoffed. "You call that crap coffee? It's more like colored water that a cow shit in then they filtered it through again."

I froze. I'd never heard O'Connor talk that way before. Sure, he gave as good as he got when it came to insults, but to blatantly curse and complain about the police department was not like him. If I hadn't felt guilty about pussyfooting around at the spa, I did now. They needed me on this case, and I'd been playing around.

"I'm back!" Mandy announced, pushing the door open with an arm full of travel cups and boxes from our favorite bakery. Her eyes found me and then Michael, the edges widening a bit. A flush covered her cheeks - no doubt remembering the time she walked in on us doing it - as she busied herself putting her boxes and cups down. "Jane. What are you doing here? And with ... Michael?" she asked it like she wasn't sure which one she was talking to.

"Amanda," Michael inclined his head, his arms crossed over his chest.

"You guys look nice," she commented, noticing my halter top and low hip pants.

"We were on a date." I leaned my butt on the edge of the table and grinned.

"Oh. Oh!" Mandy's eyes widened even further. "That's great. I'm really happy for you. But what are you doing here?"

"Exactly what I was trying to find out," O'Connor growled. He dug around in one of the bags and pulled out a large apple fritter. My stomach grumbled in protest. I knew where we were going next.

"Like I was just about to tell Mr. Grumpy Pants, I think I know who is stealing from the spa." I tried to reach for one of the donuts, but Mandy smacked my hand. I glared at her but kept my hands to myself.

"What do you mean you think?" O'Connor argued, shoving half of the apple fritter in his mouth. Hooligan. "Shouldn't you know?"

I sighed. "One, don't talk with your mouth full. Have some respect for your pastries. Two, I'm psychic. I'm not all knowing. I can only work with what I'm given."

"And what's that?" Mandy asked, taking a sip of her coffee.

"The manager," I started, causing a groan from the rest of the room. I held my hands up and frowned. "Now, hold on just hear me out. The manager didn't tell us everything we needed to know."

"So, you're not trying to pin it on him again?" O'Connor asked, surprise in his voice.

"No, I'm not doing that at all. I have another scenario in mind." I leaned forward and snatched Mandy's cup out of her hand before she could stop me. Taking a long savory drink, I sighed. Coffee. "Anyway, I learned from the maids that Riley and

Crystal had been dating until he cheated on her. They were seen fighting on more than one occasion about the thefts." Mandy took her cup back with a warning glare, her nails digging into my hand. Pursing my lips, I rubbed my hand. "She's dating the security guy Ernie now, who's in a shit ton of debt."

"Wait a second." O'Connor waved his second donut in the air. "Who's Crystal?"

"The hospitality manager."

"Okay," O'Connor answered, his brows furrowed. "And she's dating Ernie?"

"The security manager. Yes. Keep up." I snapped my fingers in front of him. "Anyway, I heard from Abigail that Ernie is a mooch and tries to beg money off anyone who will give it to him, and his latest victim is Crystal, who's the head of the maids." I stared at them trying to get them to get on my line of thinking. "Who has access to all the rooms which were stolen from?"

"Oh!" Mandy's mouth opened in a wide O. "So, you think Ernie and Crystal are working together?"

"Yes."

"Who's Abigail?" O'Connor asked, actually writing this crap down.

"One of the maids." I moved over to Michael, who had taken up residence against the wall. "You ready?"

"Now, hold up a second." Mandy moved around the table to block our paths. "You can't just drop this on us and leave. We have to figure this out."

I huffed and put my hands on my hips. "Do I have to do everything? I gave you your suspect, who has a motive, and the means to do the job. What else can I give you?"

"And you're basing this all off hearsay?" O'Connor scoffed. "I could have done that myself."

I sniffed and looked at my nails. "I doubt it. They wouldn't talk to you. You're a cop. They'll only talk to one of their own."

"Then why didn't we put you undercover as staff rather than a guest?" O'Connor countered.

"Now, let's not get hasty," I hurried to stop him from ruining everything. "I needed to get both sides. The spirits can be very fickle when they want to be. They might not have given me anything from the staff. Then I would be stuck without a way into the guest areas."

"Fine, but we're not just going to take your word for it. We'll have to look up this guy Ernie …"

O'Connor looked up from his paper waiting for me to fill in the blanks.

"Slousky."

"And Crystal?"

"Don't know it and didn't ask. I'm sure you have a list of employees somewhere. There can't be that many Crystals." I waved at their mess of papers on the desk before bypassing Mandy.

Michael stopped me and muttered something in my ear. I turned back to the two of them who had settled in for a long night. "By the way, your time-line for the murder is wrong. It'd be a two-hour time frame, not four."

Before they could ask anything else, I ducked out with Michael and headed toward the front. My phone started beeping like crazy, and I had no doubt that it was Mandy wanting me to come back. I'd done my good deed for the night, I had a date to finish.

"Now where?" Michael asked as we got into the car. He had drunk quite a lot of my blood this time, and I was happy to see that it had the desired lasting effect. I'd hate for him to disappear mid-dinner or something.

"Now, I'm starving. I want some donuts of my own, and then I want to curl up on the couch with you." I smacked my lips against Michael's before starting the car and pulling out of the parking lot. I had a lot of night left ahead of me, and I didn't want to waste it at the police station.

Besides, a date with an angel was a once-in-a-lifetime kind of thing. Who'd say no to that?

15

"Oh, yeah. That's it. Just there." I moaned into the bed, my whole body tingling with excitement. If I hadn't already been completely nude, I'd have been ripping my clothes off right then and there. I was already on the edge of orgasming. Just a little more.

"Ma'am, please stop. Or I'm going to stop," the masseuse complained again.

"No, please don't stop." I quickly lifted my head up and looked to May, my new best friend. Or at least, I was trying to make her that. However, she didn't quite have the same kind of sense of humor as Mandy did. She did have magic fingers though, that was always a plus.

"I've warned you already." Not-my-best-friend

narrowed her eyes, her white outfit a stark contrast to the darkened room. "I'm happy that you are enjoying your massage, but those kinds of sounds and comments are meant for the bedroom, not the massage table."

"I understand." I nodded, trying to look as contrite as possible. "I promise not another peep from me." I zipped my lips and laid back down on the table.

"Very well but one more and we're done." May went back to doing miraculous things to my body. The urge to declare my pleasure loudly bubbled up, but I forced it back, not wanting to lose my time. Once Mandy and O'Connor made the arrest, I was sure to lose all my spa privileges. I had to use them while I could.

"Enjoying yourself?" Lucifer's voice murmured in my ear just as I had settled into a state of euphoria.

"Very much, now go away," I hissed low, hoping May wouldn't hear me.

"I'm hurt." Lucifer pouted. If I could see him, I was sure he had pressed his hand to his chest trying to be as dramatic as possible.

"No, you're not. Go away." I muttered again, trying to get him to leave.

"What was that?" May asked, her hands pausing on my calf.

"Nothing," I said, a bit louder. "Just thinking aloud. Lots of things to do today is all."

"Okay," May said, the suspicion in her voice telling me she didn't believe me.

I swore if Lucifer ruined this for me, I'd never speak to him again.

"I can tell you are busy right now, so I'll talk. You can just listen." Lucifer started and then his face was before mine beneath the table. "I heard about your date with Michael, and I want in."

"You—"

"No, talking remember?" Lucifer put his finger up against my lips causing them to buzz.

Rolling my eyes, I sighed.

"Right, so. Michael told us about your date, and I think it's high time I took you on one of my own." He clasped his hands in front of him as he squatted before me. "I'm sure you will be utterly delighted with what I have planned. After all, it has to be better than some work party and donuts."

The utter disdain in his voice made me want to protest, but I couldn't do that right now with May in the room. Instead, I could do nothing but listen to Lucifer downplay the date I had with Michael.

It wasn't as boring as he said. We had a lovely time at the party which, of course, had been interrupted by work, but after I had reported to Mandy, we stopped and got a whole box of donuts. I spent the rest of the night showing Michael some of my favorite shows while sharing the box. Of course, donuts have icing, and that somehow ended up in naughty places that were totally not my fault, and we ended up sticky and naked in bed. Something I felt embarrassed about since I knew the people who cleaned the rooms.

Overall though, the night had been fun and satisfying in every aspect. Not that I didn't think Lucifer could show me just as good a time, but for him to try and say he could outdo it that easily was laughable. Some of the best dates were those that didn't cost an arm and a leg.

"All done," May announced, moving away from the table. I sat up slowly, grabbing the sheet to cover my chest. May wiped her hands off and nodded toward my robe. "Take your time getting dressed and please feel free to fill out a comment card for your service."

"Thanks," I muttered and waited until she left before hopping off the table. I glanced back at Lucifer, whose eyes were firmly on my barely covered form. "I'll have you know my date with Michael was perfect. Nothing you say can ruin it for me."

"You misunderstand." Lucifer came up beside me, his eyes scanning my glistening skin. "I don't wish to taint your experience with Michael, I only wish to outshine him. I am the brightest star in Heaven. It's my birthright."

"Was," I reminded him with a smirk. "You were the Morning Star. Now, you are the Lord of Hell."

"King, get it right." Lucifer's lips twisted. "Are you going to change? We should get moving if we are going to have our date. Though I'd be just as happy to stay in here with you." His fingers trailed along my bare shoulder causing tingling to shoot through my arm.

"What makes you think I want to go on a date with you right now?" I asked, moving away from him to grab my underwear. To his disappointment, I pulled them on underneath the sheet not once showing anything other than a flash of leg.

"Are you saying you don't?" Lucifer purred, blocking my path to the rest of my clothes. I could have put the robe on May had offered, but it only covered part of me, something that Lucifer would easily discard with a pull of the tie.

I sighed and shoved a hand through his middle ignoring the numbing effect it had. I grabbed my pants and then shimmied them on. "I'm not saying that. I'm saying you are presuming too much. At least Michael asked me on a date."

"My apologies, love." Lucifer bowed slightly. With how close we were, he ended up with his head in my mid-section. Talk about getting to the center of things.

I reached through him and grabbed the rest of my clothes before backing away. I turned my back to him and dropped the sheet. Surprisingly he didn't try to peek around me but waited behind. I quickly snapped my bra on and then threw my shirt on over my head.

"So …?" I twisted back around my hands on my hips and my foot tapping. "I'm waiting."

Lucifer's brow raised slightly. "Waiting? Oh, right. Jane," he started, taking a knee on the carpet, "will you do me the honor of going on a date with me this evening? Or day? Your humans' limited conception of time is so debilitating."

I looked to the heavens as if God could help me through this. "Sure. Why not? I don't have anything else to do."

Not to be swayed, Lucifer hopped to his feet

and clapped his hands together. "Great. Let's go then. Give me your blood, and we can start our date."

"No."

Lucifer frowned. "What do you mean no? Our date won't be any fun if I can't touch you. Besides, I want to try that hot sauce Michael and Gabriel keep complaining about."

"You want to try hot sauce?" I giggled, grabbing my bag. "I'm sure they told you how hot it is."

Lucifer scoffed. "I live in the bowels of Hell. Don't tell me about hot. I know hot. Some wimpy sauce made by humans is nothing." He waved it off as if it really wasn't worth his time.

"Fine, I'll get you some, but you're not gonna like it," I taunted him. "And I can't turn you corporeal in here. I came in alone. I can't very well leave with someone, now can I?"

Lucifer didn't seem happy about it but followed behind me as I left the room. I waved a hand at the front desk as I left, Lucifer hot on my heels. He followed me until I ducked into one of the private offices they had reserved in the lobby for guests to use. Plopping my bag on the desk, I dug around for the nail file I'd put in there this morning.

Grabbing it in my hand, I tried to decide where

to cut myself this time. I didn't want to cut my arm again, that had hurt like a bitch, but then again, my fingers were getting really abused.

"You know," Lucifer began, his eyes watching me, "you could always bite your tongue. I would be more than happy to heal it for you." His heated gaze made my lower half do a happy dance.

It actually wasn't a bad idea. I didn't have to risk getting an infection by whatever I was stabbing myself with, and your tongue heals faster than any other part of your body. But biting my tongue and stabbing myself were two different things entirely. Both painful but one easier to do than the other.

Scrounging up all my courage, I stuck my tongue between my teeth and bit down. Not too hard, I didn't want to bite the damn thing off, just enough for the metallic taste of blood to fill my mouth. I didn't have a chance to tell Lucifer that I'd done it before his mouth was on mine. I opened my mouth, letting his tongue dip inside, and suddenly the buzzing on my face was real solid flesh, and the hands on my face were warm and strong.

Lucifer didn't stop kissing me once he turned corporeal. He pressed me up against the desk, his hands holding my face to him. The Devil kissed me until I was breathless and couldn't think of anything but the taste and feel of him. Which was just like him. No one but him would demand all my attention that way. How he didn't die of jealousy with Michael and Gabriel sharing my bed, I didn't know.

When he finally released me, I wasn't thinking about dates anymore but about getting him naked and in my bed. Sadly, before I could do either thing, Lucifer took my hand and led me from the office, I barely had time to grab my bag before we were barreling down through the lobby.

"Where are we going?" I asked, intrigued and a bit hopeful that he had the same idea that I had. However, when we didn't head down the hallway to my room but instead into the dining room, my hopes dropped. He wanted to eat now?

"Unlike Michael, I like to do my research before a competition."

"This isn't a competition," I reminded him, trailing after him until he stopped before the door that read 'Employees Only.' "And we can't go in there."

"Sure, we can," Lucifer said with a grin that could charm the pants off your grandma. "People have been going in and out of here all day."

I tugged on his hand before he could take us in

and shook my head. "Those people work here. We don't. That's why it says employees only."

"Nonsense," Lucifer huffed. "I saw a couple come in here earlier. Which is what gave me the idea to bring you here. What's more romantic than making a meal together before we eat it?"

Before I could protest further, he had dragged me into the kitchen. It was between meal times, so it wasn't that busy. A few bus boys were stacking dishes in the dishwasher, and someone in a chef's hat was stirring something over the stove. Whatever it was smelled delicious and I was suddenly on board with Lucifer's idea.

"Excuse me." Lucifer released me and held his hands up in the air. "My lovely lady here and I are hungry and would like to make a meal to eat together." He tucked his hands into his pockets and swung around to grin at me before adding, "And if anyone has a problem with that you can take it up with me. Lucifer. The Devil."

I crossed my arm under the other and placed my face in my palm. I didn't want to see these people's reaction. I didn't need this kind of excitement in my life right now. Really, what had he been thinking?

When there wasn't an immediate call for our

dismissal, I slowly lifted my face to see everyone completely ignoring us. I stepped up beside Lucifer and stared in awe.

The cook at the stove came over to us, threw us a pair of aprons and said with a Latino accent, "Don't break anything," before he went back to his business.

"What happened? Why aren't they throwing us out?" I put the apron over my head and tied it around my waist.

Lucifer beamed as he did the same and led me over to the counter. "You keep forgetting, love. I'm the Devil. Getting people to do what I want is what I do."

16

"So, what are you in the mood for?" Lucifer started pulling things down from the shelves in front of us. A bowl. A knife. A spatula. Which he promptly smacked me on the ass with.

"Um, well, I guess it depends on what we have to work with. You said you wanted to try something with hot sauce on it, so maybe we should make something we can put that on." I glanced around the counter for other things we might need.

"And what kind of food would that be?" Lucifer asked, genuinely curious to know. I'd never met a man who listened as much as these guys did. Really, it was like they were hanging on every word. While it was good in some ways, I also had to watch what

I said because I had a tendency to embarrass myself and these guys heard everything.

"Well, you can do anything really. Gabriel ate it on burritos and Michael did it with eggs. But you can also put it on chicken or pasta."

Lucifer snapped his fingers and pointed at me. "That. Let's do that."

"What?"

"Pasta." Lucifer grabbed a huge pot, large enough I could fit in it if I sat down.

I laughed and put my hand on his arm. "Hold up. How much are you planning on making? That pot would feed the whole hotel."

"No, it wouldn't," the lone cook still stirring his pot said over his shoulder. "A dozen or so people but not the whole hotel. Believe me, I've done it."

"Good tip." I glanced back at him and then asked, "What's your name?"

"Jose."

"Hi, Jose. I'm Ja-Patty." I caught myself before giving my real name. There was already too much confusion as it was. I offered him my hand, but he seemed reluctant to take it. Eventually, he did give it a small shake. "This is Lucifer, as you already know." I pointed back at my angel still gathering up supplies we didn't really need.

"Is he really the Devil?" Jose asked, nodding his head in Lucifer's direction.

"Sure, I am." Lucifer finally stopped long enough to turn around and answer. "I can read into your very soul. Tell you your darkest secrets."

Jose blanched, and I giggled nervously. "Oh, don't mind him. He's a bit dramatic. You can hardly blame him when his parents named him after the literal Devil."

My words made Jose relax slightly but not much. Instead, he turned back to his pot and kept glancing our way every once in a while.

I smacked Lucifer on the arm. "Now, look what you did. I was trying to make friends, and you scared him."

Lucifer gave me a sideways look. "You really think I'm dramatic?"

"Yes."

"I'm far from dramatic. I just like to add a bit of flair to everyday life. Makes things more interesting." He grinned wolfishly.

"So, you call rebelling against Heaven adding flair?" I asked, moving away from the table to where the dry foods were kept. I found a box of pasta noodles and brought it back to the table. "Or how about this whole 'I have to have a better date than Michael' business? That's not dramatic?"

Lucifer took the noodles from me and put them in the pot. "First off, wanting to beat that 'I'm better than everyone' douche is not being dramatic." I rolled my eyes, and he put up two fingers. "Secondly, I didn't rebel against Heaven so much as move out of my father's house. Humans do it all the time."

"There's a difference," I argued. Lucifer started to stir the pasta in the pot, and I sighed. "You need water, or the noodles won't soften." I took the pot from him and took it over to the sink.

Turning on the faucet, I glanced over at the busboys who were busy working on the dishes. They smiled shyly, but when they saw Lucifer come up behind me, their smiles dropped.

"How do you know how much water to add?" Lucifer looked over my shoulder while I waited for the pot to fill.

"You need enough to cover the noodles. It doesn't matter a whole lot in any case. You won't be keeping the water. It's just so you can boil it." I tried to pick the pot up, but it was a bit heavier than the one I had at home.

"Here." Lucifer bumped me out of the way and

lifted the pot out of the sink. "Wow, that is quite heavy." He held it in front of him as he shuffled across the room.

"To the stove, not the counter," I instructed him before he could set it down.

Huffing in effort, Lucifer placed the pot down hard enough that water sloshed over the side, making the stove hiss and Jose glare. Lucifer shrugged a shoulder. "What? I'm an angel. I've never cooked before."

Jose just shook his head and went to grab something from the pantry. I moved over to where Lucifer stood and picked up a large, clean black spoon. "Here, move the noodles around, so they don't get stuck to the sides. You also want to put some salt in there and turn the burner on."

"How do I do that?" Lucifer bent down to where the knobs were and stared at them like they were an alien life form.

I pointed at the knob in front of our burner. "That one will turn it on. Now, be sure to stand back because this is an industrial stove and I don't want you to - ah!" I cried out when Lucifer turned on the stove without doing what I said, and a large flame spouted out from beneath the pot, singeing the Devil quite good.

"Holy mother of - fuck!" Lucifer grabbed his face and jerked to a standing position. There goes the idea that they couldn't get hurt while corporeal, though we'd already established that with Michael's couch incident.

"Are you okay?" I asked, reaching for him. I turned him to face me, and the moment I saw his face, I forced my mouth shut.

"What?" Lucifer touched his face. "Is it bad? I've never been burnt before, so I don't exactly know how it feels. Angel, you know."

I shook my head and clamped my fist over my mouth. I tried really hard not to laugh, I did. But when the Devil stood before you with only one eyebrow, it was hard not to laugh.

"Why are you laughing?" Lucifer frowned, his brows furrowing, but with only one there, it looked even more ridiculous, causing me to laugh harder. "What? What is it?"

Jose came back in that instant and saw Lucifer's face. He burst out laughing, pointing a finger and smacking his thigh. "You only have one eyebrow. You look so loco, eh?"

Lucifer's eyes widened, and he searched for something to see himself in. "I'm missing an eyebrow? How could you not tell me I'm missing an eyebrow?" He grabbed a shiny silver pot and held it up to his face, moving his head one way and then the other, trying to see his face clearly.

I shook my head and laughed. "I'm sorry. I just didn't want you to feel bad."

"Well, I feel bloody brilliant now," Lucifer snapped, shooting daggers my way with his eyes.

I slid in behind him and stroked along the missing brow. "It's fine. No one will notice. And I bet when you turn back, it'll regrow."

"You think?" Lucifer asked, his voice almost hopeful.

Nodding, I leaned my face on his shoulder. "Positive. After all, you can change your appearance at will. I doubt an eyebrow will be much of a challenge."

Straightening out, Lucifer nodded. "You're right. It will be fine. Now, let's finish making our pasta."

"You still want to?" I gaped. "After all that?"

"Pfft. You think a bit of a singeing will put me off? I wanted to have a meal with you that we created, and I'm going to do exactly that." He moved back over to our pot and looking at the top. "Now, what's next?"

Chewing on my lower lip, I thought about what

we needed. "Well, I find hot sauce tastes best with chicken pasta. So, we'll want to make a cream sauce of some kind."

Lucifer slapped his hands together eager to get started. "Alright, point me in the direction of the sauce."

"Well, there are several things we need." I started to list them in my head as I walked over to the pantry. My eyes landed on a jar, and I came back out and handed it to Lucifer. "Here. Probably best we don't try and make it from scratch tonight. I think we've had enough adventures."

Lucifer took the jar of pasta sauce from me and stared down at it. "This is cream sauce? It looks like something a demon barfed up."

"Trust me, it's sauce." I grimaced at the imagery Lucifer had put in my head. Demon. Barf. Yuck.

"So, what do I do with this?" Lucifer moved over to the stove and undid the cap. "Do I pour it into the noodles?"

He started to tip the jar when everyone in the kitchen shouted, "No!"

Lucifer froze and straightened the jar. Jose snatched it from his hand and started saying something in Spanish I didn't understand, but I was pretty sure he was cursing out Lucifer and calling his mama some bad names. Jose turned to me and shoved the jar in my hands.

"Don't let this one cook," Jose warned before taking his pot off the stove and going to the counter.

Smacking my lips together impatiently, I grabbed a saucepan and put it on the abandoned burner. I poured the sauce into the pan and turned the burner back on to low.

"Can I trust you to stir?" I asked, holding a spoon out to Lucifer with a warning look.

Lucifer made a disgusted sound in the back of his throat. "Of course, I can stir. What, do I look like an idiot?" I stifled a snort laugh, but it escaped my hand. Lucifer growled and jerked the spoon from my hands. "Don't answer that."

Clearing my throat, I shook my head. "I'm sorry. Really, I am, but I have to say this is turning out to be a better date than I had with Michael. Definitely more entertaining."

"Really?" Lucifer's eyes brightened. "You're not just saying that because I burnt my eyebrow off, are you?"

"Of course, I am." I grinned cheekily, earning me a pinch. "Hey. Don't be a spoil sport."

"I'll show you spoil sport," Lucifer warned, abandoning his stirring to grab me around the waist. He drew me up to him, his mouth stroking mine lovingly. I sank into his embrace with a sigh and then something popped next to us.

"Lucifer, the sauce!" I pushed him away and back toward the stove where the sauce had begun to bubble. "Pay attention. If we burn the sauce, then it's all over. Don't forget to stir the noodles every once in a while, too."

Lucifer pursed his lips together and asked, "What are you going to do?"

"I'm going to the fridge to look for some chicken. We probably should have done that first, but I wasn't thinking clearly." I grinned backing away from him. "I blame you for that."

Smirking with male satisfaction, Lucifer placed his hand on his chest. "I'll take that blame gladly."

Giggling like a school girl, I went to the walk-in fridge and looked for chicken. Sandwich meat. Hot dogs. Eggs. No chicken.

I turned around in a circle and tried to think of what we could use instead of chicken. It wouldn't be horrible to use the sandwich meat. I mean it was ham, but still, it was still meat. Then again, the hot dogs could work as well. Just as I was about to grab the hot dogs, I caught sight of a box labeled chicken further into the fridge.

The box was stuck between two other ones, and I struggled to get the top one off the box I needed. The box tilted to one side and before I could stop it, the box fell off. I jumped to the side just barely missing being squashed by a box of what looked like watermelons.

"Really?" I exclaimed, kicking one of them with my foot. "Who puts watermelons in a box? And next to the chicken? That's a health violation if I ever saw one." I bent down to pick up the watermelons and grumbling to myself. My hand reached for another melon and landed on a black shoe. Grasping the shoe firmly, I frowned. Shoes don't belong in the fridge.

I tried to pull it out to show Jose, but it was stuck. I tugged on it and then reached down to see what it was caught on only to find a long hard leg attached to it. Swallowing hard, I tried to calm the rapid beating of my heart as I moved the cart in front of the leg to the side.

"It's just someone taking a nap," I reassured myself. As the cart moved and the pale unseeing eyes of a man wearing a security guard outfit came into view, I couldn't deny it any longer.

The guy was dead. And not just dead dead, but dead for a while dead. I sighed and checked the name tag. Just my luck.

"Oh, Ernie. What have you gotten yourself into?" I asked the dead guy in front of me as I pulled my phone from my back pocket and dialed Mandy. She was not going to be happy about this.

17

L eaning against the counter with Lucifer, I rubbed my hand over my face. Considering the dead guy in the fridge, we decided to postpone our date. Besides, Lucifer had burnt the sauce beyond repair. I guess that was what I get for giving him more than one responsibility at a time.

"Are you alright?" Lucifer asked, putting his arm around my shoulders.

I leaned into his embrace and shook my head. "No, not really." I paused for a moment, the sight of Ernie's cold body still in the forefront of my mind. "I had expected to see a dead body from time to time in this field. I mean, dead bodies must be every day for Mandy and them, but I didn't expect to find one in the fridge."

Lucifer pressed his forehead to the side of my face. "It's hard, I know. I wish I could tell you it gets easier, but it doesn't. Every time it happens, it will be a fight to keep your sanity."

I glanced up at him to see a dark expression had covered his face. "Is that what it's like in Hell? Having to see all those people in constant torment?"

Shaking his head, Lucifer smiled, but it was forced. "No, it is worse, but then again, God didn't put me in that position because it was easy."

I started to ask him something else, but a commotion outside the kitchen door stopped me. I glanced around the room, to see Jose and the busboys tense. I had a feeling they didn't really want the cops in their kitchen.

"B.F.P.D," Mandy announced, pushing through the doors of the kitchen. She flashed her badge around the room. Her eyes moved to Lucifer and me, and her face scrunched in confusion.

"Hey," I nodded to her, straightening. "Where's O'Connor?"

I had barely gotten the words out before

O'Connor came through the door, flashing his badge and his gun liberally.

"Okay, what have we got here?" O'Connor demanded, his eyes immediately going to Jose. "Do I need to arrest someone? I'm in an arresting mood. Give me a reason."

"O'Connor," Mandy warned rolling her eyes. "Jane called."

"I thought your name was Patty?" Jose asked, and then tensed when O'Connor got in his face. "That's what she said."

"Right," Mandy agreed. "Sorry, I must have heard your name wrong on the call."

Apparently, we were pretending they didn't know me. The way Mandy's eyes kept going to Lucifer and the way he held me, we weren't pretending that much. I could see the question on her tongue, but she refrained.

"He's in there." I gestured with my head toward the fridge. "I didn't move anything. Well, except the box of watermelons that I knocked over before I found him."

"Watermelons?" O'Connor asked, moving away from Jose causing him to let out a breath. "Why would anyone put watermelons in a box?"

"What I thought exactly!" I pointed a hand at

him. "How was that smart? Plus, they were on top of a box of chicken. Not safe."

O'Connor shot Jose a disgusted look. "I will be having the health department down here after we have finished up here."

"Don't look at me." Jose held his hands up in defense. "I'm just the backup chef. I don't run the kitchen."

I snorted but didn't say anything. No wonder he didn't care if we used it. He probably didn't give a rat's ass about us being there. Except maybe the fact that we almost blew up the stove. That he might have gotten in trouble for.

"Get me the resort manager, Riley Parks," O'Connor demanded, jerking his head toward the door. Jose scrambled to obey, more than happy to be out of there. I could sympathize with him. I didn't want to be there either.

"Alright, let's get this over with." O'Connor started toward the fridge but then paused in front of Lucifer. He glanced between us and then asked, "I thought you were dating that one large blonde fellow. Mike."

"Michael," I corrected. God forbid he hear O'Connor call him that. I didn't need another drama queen on my hands. "And I was. I mean I am. I'm also dating Lucifer."

O'Connor's brow rose up, and a strange smile covered his face. "Really now? And how do you feel about this?" he asked Lucifer.

Lucifer pulled me closer to him and smirked. "I'm good. There's plenty of … Patty" - he glanced down at me for confirmation, and I nodded - "to go around."

The detective chuckled as if he had just heard a good joke before shaking his head and rubbing his jaw. O'Connor walked over to the fridge and opened it. Mandy shot me a look, telling me we'd be talking about Lucifer later, before following O'Connor into the fridge.

Lucifer and I waited while they did whatever the hell they did, none of us speaking. They were only in there for a few minutes before they came back out, cleaning their hands on some wet wipes Mandy had magically produced.

"You call it in, I want to talk to our witnesses here for a moment." Mandy inclined her head toward O'Connor, who for once didn't argue with her. When O'Connor was gone, she turned to the bus boys. "Did you see anyone come in here? Anything suspicious?"

"No," the first busboy said.

"No way. We didn't get here until about an hour ago, right before those two came in." The other one pointed a finger at Lucifer and me.

"Right," Mandy nodded. "Well, then you're free to go, but give your contact information to O'Connor before you leave."

The two busboys took off, not once looking back at us. Cowards.

"So." Mandy pulled a notepad out of her pocket, her pen poised. "First off, this is Lucifer? He doesn't look like the Devil. Shouldn't he have like horns?" She stared at Lucifer's head a bit fearfully. Which I found funny because even being Catholic like she was, she didn't even believe in the Devil or Hell.

Lucifer chuckled. "The horn thing was so last millennia. I try to go for a more approachable look nowadays. It certainly made it easier to attract this one." He stroked my chin with his thumb, a soft smile on his lips.

Mandy stared at us and slowly let out a sigh. "Right. So, then what were you guys doing here? I thought the case was closed? We were going to arrest Ernie and Crystal."

I snorted. "Good luck with that." Mandy looked

at me curiously. "That's Ernie in there. You didn't check the name tag?"

Mandy had the good sense to duck her head, busying herself with writing on her notepad. "So, you just found him like that? Nothing out of the ordinary."

"Not besides the watermelons." I shrugged. "We were making dinner, and we needed chicken, so I went to the fridge and boom there he was." I smacked my hands together. "Well, not boom. He didn't magically appear. Or at least, I don't think so. But I went to pick the watermelons up, and I found his shoe. Apparently, that shoe had an owner, and it was still attached to him." I waved a hand at her. "Then I called you."

"Why were you making dinner here?" she asked with an arched eyebrow. "You have an apartment."

"Uh." I ducked my head for a second. "Well, I wanted to make sure to get my massage in before I had to check out. You know, I'll never get another chance. Not with what I'm making."

"Jane," Mandy growled, shaking her head, "you are using city money for that. You can't go spending it all willy-nilly."

I giggled. Willy-nilly. "Fine. I'm sorry, but I had

to after I spent all day cleaning the rooms here, I needed a bit of relaxation."

"Cleaning the rooms? When did you do that?" Mandy asked, her face scrunched up.

"The other day but that's beside the point." I moved out of Lucifer's embrace to point at Mandy's notepad. "The critical point is why do you have a notepad? You have a phone for a reason. Take notes on that."

Mandy pulled the notepad away from my grasp and grumbled, "I can't work the stupid thing."

I gasped. "You can't work your smartphone? That's it. I must revoke your cool card. You are no longer a member of my generation. I'd expect that from O'Connor, he's like fifty, but you?" I shook my head and tisked. "Just shameful."

Lucifer chuckled behind me.

"Leave me alone," Mandy snapped. "And O'Connor is thirty-five, not fifty. Stop exaggerating."

"Fine, but seriously, who do you think killed Ernie? Crystal?" I crossed my arms over my chest and tried to think who would have the motive.

"I guess." Mandy tapped her pen on her notepad. "We don't really know anything about him besides the debt. I mean, unless there's someone he stole a lot of money from. Maybe they did it."

"Well, Abigail did say that he was mooching off Crystal a lot. Maybe she finally got tired of it. Or maybe she caught him stealing from the guests?" I started throwing ideas out there, not really knowing what actually happened.

"It's possible, but we'll have to find out his cause of death before we can do anything. There weren't any lacerations or gunshot wounds, no apparent reason for his death." Mandy tucked her notepad into her pocket and sighed. "We'll know more when the M.E. gets a hold of him."

"Okay." I moved back over to Lucifer and took his hand. "Well, we'll be in my room. Just let me know when you want me to go interrogate Crystal."

Mandy grabbed my arm. "No, you're not going to go near her. We can't risk you tipping her off. And you need to check out. The case is over. We'll take it from here."

"But Mandy," I whined, "it's close to bedtime. At least let me stay one more night. I promise I'll check out in the morning."

Mandy growled and finally released me. "Fine. One more night, but you better not mess anything up or charge any more to the room, or I'll make sure it comes out of your check."

"Fine. Fine." I held my hands up, waving her off. "I'll only eat what's in the mini fridge."

"No mini fridge!" she shouted after me, and I ignored her, bolting with Lucifer out the door.

We bypassed O'Connor who shouted after us, "No running!" and then we were down the hall and into my room. Kicking my shoes off, I immediately headed to the mini-fridge and pulled out everything.

"Alright, let's see what we got here." I began to sort the goods out into drinks and snacks. "So, we have a bunch of shots if you're looking to get your first hangover." I waved one of the little bottles of liqueur in Lucifer direction.

He reached out to take it from my hand, but when I let it go, it fell to the ground. Luckily, it was carpeted, and the bottle didn't break, but I was still bummed. Lucifer's solid form had worn off.

"Well, that sucks." I leaned down to pick up the bottle. "I was hoping we had more time."

Lucifer sighed. "I did too. We didn't even get to eat our meal."

"You mean our burnt meal." I pointed out with

a raised brow. "Hey, your eyebrow is back. That's a plus."

Lucifer touched his face and grinned. "Well, that's one less thing to worry about."

I fiddled with the bottle of liqueur and looked up at him from beneath my lashes, suddenly a bit shy. "You know, I could just give you some more blood. Then you would be corporeal again, and we can finish our date."

Moving closer to me, Lucifer reached out, but then his hand stopped mid-air. His head tilted to the side for a moment before he cursed. "I'm sorry, I have to go. It seems like there is some sort of emergency." He growled and glared up at the ceiling. "One that conveniently happened in the middle of our date!"

Frowning at how upset he was getting, I tried to lighten the mood. "Don't worry about it. It's not like you're going anywhere. We can finish our date another time. Besides, I really shouldn't be getting into the mini fridge. Mandy wasn't lying about taking it out of my check."

Lucifer didn't seem convinced by my words but didn't argue. He stroked along the side of my face, leaving zings of electricity in its wake before disappearing.

Sighing, I glanced at the pile of food on the counter and then started to shove it back into the fridge. I'd just order a pizza or something. I'd gotten everything but the little bottles into the fridge when I stopped. Ernie's dead eyes stared back at me and suddenly being alone didn't seem like a good idea.

"Fuck it." I gathered the bottles up in my arms and plopped down on the couch. Twisting the top off the first one, I downed it in one go. I'd just started on the second one when someone pounded on the door.

"Jane, I'm coming in. You better not be naked in there." The door handle jiggled, but she didn't open it right away.

"Nope!" I called out, already getting a bit buzzed. "No naked people in here. Just little ole me." I giggled and played with the tiny bottle in my hand.

Mandy opened the door and took one look at me before stomping across the room. "What did I tell you?" She snatched the tiny bottle from my hand before I could drink it.

"Hey! I was going to drink that." I scrambled for the others before she could take them.

"No, you don't. And where's Lucifer?" she

looked around the room as if he were hiding somewhere.

I tipped another bottle back and giggled, "He had to go. Some emergency."

"In Hell?"

"Or Heaven. Who knows? I didn't ask."

"And he left you here by yourself? After finding a dead body like that?" Mandy clucked her tongue and shook her head. Moving around the couch, she plopped down next to me. "Move over and give me one of those."

I tossed her a tiny bottle and grinned as she downed it. "Welcome to Chateau de Jane."

18

I woke the next morning with a foot in my face and an elbow in my back. How that was possible could only be explained by Mandy's weird sleeping habits.

And the snoring.

I shoved the foot away and rolled out of bed, a movement I instantly regretted. My stomach rolled, and I rushed to the bathroom.

After I emptied my stomach in the toilet, I turned the cold water on in the sink. I soaked a cloth in the water and then wiped it over my face and the back of my neck.

Staring at my reflection in the mirror, I didn't like what I saw. My face was so pale that a vampire coven was probably looking for me to join their ranks. My hair had seen better days. It didn't have that usual lustrous glow but lay dull and lifeless around my face.

This is the face that angels adore. I scoffed at the thought. The only thing adoring this face today would be the shower and my pillow.

I twisted toward the shower and turned it on. Pulling my shirt over my head, I didn't even bother wondering where my pants had gone last night. Mandy and I had gotten so plastered that I was lucky I had clothes on at all.

Stepping under the spray, I let out a pleasurable sigh. Hot water was a miraculous thing. How anyone ever survived without it before, I'd never know. I knew I couldn't. No Middle Ages for me, no boiling water just to fill a tub.

I'd never really thought much about what Heaven looked like, but now that I've met angels I could clearly see it. It was me in a clawfoot bathtub full of warm water with all three of my angels surrounding me. They fed me strawberries and offered me a glass of champagne, while the third one rubbed my shoulders. No! My feet. Okay, so they could rub another part of me that had started to wake up during my little fantasy.

My fingers trailed down my stomach and

slipped between my thighs. I had only just started to relieve my need when a pounding on the door stopped me. I peeked out the shower door and cocked my head to the side. The pounding wasn't in the room, it was from outside the room.

Growling, I jumped out of the shower and wrapped a towel around me. When I got out of the bathroom, I could clearly hear O'Connor yelling from the other side of the door.

Stomping through the bedroom, I smacked Mandy's sleeping head as I passed. "Get up, sleepy head. Your wakeup call is here."

Not caring that I was only in a towel, I opened the door. Looking the detective up and down with a frown, I said, "You're not the strippers I called."

"Ha, ha, very funny." O'Connor put his hands on his hips and scowled. "Is Stevenson in there?"

"Mandy, are you in here?" I yelled over my shoulder. A groan was my only response. "It seems like she's still alive. Lucky for you."

O'Connor tried to investigate the room over my shoulder, but I blocked his view. "What are you doing?" he growled.

"Keeping you from embarrassing you and Mandy. I don't know what kind of state she's in right now, but I think it's probably best if you wait for us in the Lobby."

He tried to glance over my shoulder one more time, but I moved into his view again. Frowning, he straightened up and brushed a hand over his nose. "Fine, be there in five minutes. Not a minute more."

I sighed. "It's no wonder your wife divorced you." I gestured to my towel clad form. "This takes more than five minutes to put together. Any guy would know that."

O'Connor gnashed his teeth at me, stepping into my personal space to poke a finger at my chest. "Don't ever talk about my wife again."

"Ex-wife," I reminded him. "And O'Connor, if you wanted to see me naked all you had to do was ask." I smirked down at his finger at the top of my towel. I reached up and pretended like I was going to undo it.

O'Connor's face reddened, and he immediately removed his finger, turning on his heel and shouting over his shoulder. "Twenty minutes, Stevenson!"

Chuckling to myself, I closed the door on him. Mandy came stumbling out of the bedroom, only half dressed as well. "Who was that?"

"Your partner. Don't worry, I sent him on his

way." I moved over to my bag and pulled out my last pair of clean underwear. I probably should have done laundry. Or brought more clothes. Either way, at least I was leaving today, so it didn't really matter.

"Please tell me you didn't answer the door like that?" She grimaced at my towel ensemble.

"Okay, I didn't." I smiled over my shoulder before standing. "Don't worry, I didn't mess with O'Connor ... much."

Mandy shook her head and tugged her bedhead into a high ponytail. "I swear, one of these days he's going to pull a gun on you, and I'm not going to do anything to stop him."

"Oh, yes, you would." I pouted, and came over and hugged her. "You love me too much to let that mean old meanie kill me."

Mandy snorted and patted my arm. "I didn't say you'd die, just get maimed a bit."

"Fine, then my angel boyfriends will come kick his ass." I pushed off her and dropped my towel.

"Jane!" Mandy jerked her head the other way.

"What?" I shimmied into my underwear. "It's not like you haven't seen it all before."

"Still, give a girl some warning. I was face first to Jane ass. Not something I want to see first thing in the morning. And you better keep your angels away from my work."

Slipping on my bra, I laughed. "Hard to do that when they are my ticket to the whole being a psychic thing."

"Also, what's up with you and Lucifer going on a date? I don't see the Devil doing that." Jane moved into the bathroom, her voice becoming muffled. "While we're on the topic. Have you asked him about Hell? Is it a real thing? Cause the priest and all the nuns have been telling me for years that Hell is just your guilt trying to make you do what is right."

I finished getting dressed and then followed her to the bathroom. Leaning against the bathroom wall, I laughed. "You've now met the actual Devil, and you still doubt the existence of Hell? The Pope would be so proud."

Mandy flipped me off before shoving me out of the bathroom. "Now, if you don't mind, I'm going to wash last night off, and unlike you, I don't like an audience."

"I don't need an audience," I told the closed bathroom door. "I can't help that your partner has no sense of timing or humor. He really needs to lighten up."

"His wife left him. What do you expect?" Mandy's muffled voice said through the door. "Imagine your three guys suddenly leaving you one day. How devastated would you feel? I doubt you would be in a good mood either."

I frowned. The thought bothered me. I'd gotten so used to the three of them being around, it was hard to imagine that they would ever not be there. It made something in my chest tighten.

Instead of thinking about it, I started to pack my bag up. If I was being forced to leave today, I might as well. Not like I had anything better to do.

I finished packing up long before Mandy came out of the bathroom. She had put back on her clothes from last night. Rubbing a towel in her hair, she picked up her phone and frowned.

"What? Your latest conquest not texting you back?" I teased her.

Mandy gave me an exasperated look before tucking her phone into her back pocket. "Like that'd ever happen. No, it was O'Connor bitching about getting down there so we could arrest Crystal."

"You're going to do it now? You don't even know if she did it." I threw back over my shoulder, and shoved my feet into my shoes. "Can you really arrest her?"

Mandy shrugged, putting her badge and gun on. "She's the only suspect we have right now. We can hold her for twenty-four hours, hopefully long enough for the M.E. to get back to us about the cause of death. You said it yourself, she has a motive. If I found out my boyfriend was only with me to pay off his debts, then I'd be pretty pissed too."

"Enough to murder him?" I cocked a brow and held the room door open for her.

Mandy smirked. "Hey, don't think that just because I'm a cop means I can't commit a crime of passion."

I snorted. "It's not passion if it's premeditated."

"Semantics." Mandy pushed past me and into the hallway. "What are you going to do?"

Closing the door behind us, I lifted a shoulder. "I don't know. I quit the bar, so I'll probably go by Gotcha! and see if I have any messages. Or take a nap. Either or."

"You quit the bar?" Mandy asked, her face scrunched in confusion. "When'd this happen?"

"Uh, the night you came in to tell me about this job. I thought I told you?" I tapped my chin with my finger. "Maybe that was Lucifer. I don't know. I'm not used to having so many people to talk to. It's hard to keep up with who I told stuff to."

Mandy rolled her eyes. "Where are your boyfriends anyway? Lately, it seems like they're always around and visible."

"You noticed that, huh?" I grinned, extremely proud of myself. "Lucifer had some emergency last night like I said, and the others I haven't seen in a few. Which means one of them is bound to show up—"

"Hey," Gabriel popped out of nowhere and matched my and Mandy's stride.

"Speak of the angel." I beamed up at him. "Where've you been?"

"Which one is it?" Mandy asked, searching around for Gabriel.

"Gabriel," I told her before turning back to him. "I haven't seen you in a while."

Gabriel shrugged. "Been busy. I don't just get to spend time with you, you know."

I frowned at his tone of voice. Gabriel rarely ever gave me lip. Not the non-physical kind anyway. It bothered me, it was almost like he didn't want to talk about what he'd been doing.

"Does this have anything to do with the emergency Lucifer got called away for?" I waved a finger at him, narrowing my eyes into slits.

A forced smile crept up his face, and I knew the next words out of his mouth were going to be a lie. Could angels lie? It didn't seem like they should be able to.

"No, nothing like that. Just lots of things going on."

I glanced at him sideways but didn't pry anymore. The fact that he hadn't told me meant it was something important. I wanted to ask more but didn't want to push him. He'd tell me when he was ready.

We entered the lobby and found O'Connor and a couple of officers waiting with the manager, Riley Parks. When they saw us, O'Connor started toward us, an angry jerking movement in his stance.

"Took you long enough." O'Connor shot us a glare before looking to Mandy. "We're ready to go get Crystal. Are you done having your girls' night?"

Mandy shifted uncomfortably. "Sorry about that. I just needed to blow off some steam."

O'Connor for once didn't make a rude comment. Instead, he nodded his head as if he understood. "Just, next time, give me a heads up."

"Got it."

It was interesting to watch the two of them interact like this. Most of the time Mandy was trying not to get on O'Connor's bad side, and other times she seemed not to give a rat's ass. O'Connor was a wild card. The fact that he'd been so understanding rather than blowing up on her was a miracle. I just prayed it lasted.

We followed O'Connor as he gathered the officers he'd brought. Parks led the way into the room where I knew the maids gathered in the morning. I started to inch back, not wanting any of them to see me with the cops and think I'd betrayed them.

When I didn't enter after them, Mandy held the door and asked, "What are you doing? This was your case. Don't you want to see the big arrest?"

I shook my head, my ponytail whipping me in the face. "Nope, I'm good. It's all you."

Mandy pursed her lips but didn't argue the fact. The door shut behind her and I leaned against the wall next to it, listening for any raised voices.

"How was your date with Lucifer?" Gabriel asked, his voice low as he tried to act as if he didn't care.

I glanced up at him, tilting my head to one side. "It was going well until we found the dead body in the fridge. Then he went incorporeal, and you called him back for something."

Gabriel rubbed the back of his neck and had a guilty look on his face. "Sorry about that. It wasn't my fault, I swear." I nodded, not completely believing him, but I wasn't going to try and pry it out of him. After a moment, he said, "So, the dead body? Who was that?"

"The security guard, Ernie."

Some yelling came from the room behind me, and I straightened up. I stood back as the door slammed open and revealed the two officers trying to restrain Crystal.

She yanked at her arms, already in cuffs, and yelled, "I didn't kill Ernie. Why would I kill my own boyfriend?"

"Well, we have a security tape that says other-wise," O'Connor said coming out of the room. He glanced my way with a curious look before following the officers out.

When Mandy came out, I stopped her. "You have a security tape showing her killing Ernie?"

Mandy frowned. "No, we have a security tape of her and Ernie arguing, and she hit him. It's not enough to get a conviction but enough to bring her in whether she wants to or not."

Gabriel moved up beside me. "It wasn't her."

"Huh?" I turned my head to him. "What do you mean?"

His eyes had that far off distance look in them, and I knew he had a vision. "The person who killed Ernie was smaller than that woman. Scrawny build. I couldn't see their face, only the back of them."

"What does the back of them look like?" I asked, hoping for something to work with.

"What's he saying?" Mandy asked, her eyes going toward the front door and then back to us. I could tell she was antsy to get out of there, but not enough to miss what Gabriel had to say.

"He doesn't think it was Crystal," I told her. I paused as Riley Parks came out of the room they had been in.

He glanced at Mandy and then to me, a scowl on his face. "I presume your time here is finished?"

"Yes," Mandy answered, offering him a polite smile. "Thank you for your cooperation in this matter."

"I'm just happy we found the thief before this got leaked out to the press." Riley sniffed, adjusting his suit.

"Well, I'm sure we'll have it all cleared up soon," she explained. "I'm not sure about getting the stolen items back though. If Ernie was the thief, then unless he told Crystal, we're out of luck."

"That's fine. Just get her out of my resort." He waved a hand at me as if my very presence disgusted him.

"We're leaving now," Mandy assured him.

Riley didn't bother to say good-bye. He marched to the front and started rifling through things at the reception desk. Every few seconds, he looked up from the desk to stare at us as if that would make us leave sooner.

"Anyway, back to Gabriel. What was he saying?" Mandy asked, leading me through the Lobby and outside.

I stopped at her car and leaned against it, tucking my hands into my pockets. "He says it wasn't her. She doesn't fit the profile of the person he saw killing Ernie."

Mandy smacked her lips together. "Well, I don't know what to tell you, Jane. We can't go off some vision an angel had. We need more than that."

I glanced at Gabriel who stood behind her. "Anything else you can add?"

He focused for a moment and then shook his head. "No, I can't tell if they are male or female, only that they don't have the same build as Crystal, and there's no way she could have faked it. Her hips are too big."

I quirked a brow at his description. Really, that's what he was basing it off. Men. To Mandy, I said, "He says the person who killed Ernie is smaller, like in the hips."

"Any clue how he died?" Mandy asked, glancing down at her phone.

"They shoved a pillow over his face." Gabriel stared down at the ground as if the death really bothered him.

"He said suffocation."

"Okay," Mandy sighed, and put her phone away. "Well, there's nothing I can do until we get confirmation from the M.E. and talk to Crystal. Why don't you just go home or wherever, and I'll call you when we need you."

As I watched her get in her car and drive away, I suddenly felt irritated. They had asked me into this case and now they weren't going to listen to me? How's that for gratitude.

Turning to Gabriel, I asked, "So, what should we do?"

This time, Gabriel gave me a genuine smile, the kind that made his eyes sparkle and my panties wet. "How about a date?"

19

"Are you sure this is what you want to do on our date?" I asked Gabriel, my nose scrunched up as I tried not to take in the smell of feet and stale beer. It almost felt like I was back at the bar and not in the middle of the bowling alley.

The strobe lights blinked over us, the pounding of the music making my body hum with energy. Kids were shouting and chasing each other as their parents hollered at them to behave. It was like I'd gone back in time. to a time where there were no crimes. Only fun.

Gabriel was one of those fun things. Just standing there watching him in his jeans and button up shirt, I only felt happy. Which was how Gabriel made me feel pretty much all of the time. Happy. Out of my element. So, his choice of dates shouldn't have surprised me, but it did, something else that made me like him all the more.

"Yes." Gabriel grinned, his eyes taking in everything around him. Who'd have known bowling alleys would be so exciting to an angel? The last time I was excited about bowling, I had pigtails and couldn't bowl without the bumpers. That was only a few months ago, but still. Lucifer sure as hell wouldn't have suggested bowling.

No. Don't compare them, Jane. They are each different people. It's not right for me to compare them.

I scurried to find my enthusiasm and put on an eager face. "Alright, if bowling is what you want to do then, that's what we're doing. Let's go."

Starting over to the counter, I waved over the cashier. A woman with black and green hair came over looking as happy to be there as half the other people there. The strobe lights sparkled off her nose ring and almost blinded me. I had the urge to tell her to put her nose bling away but didn't think that would come across well. I wanted to go on this date, didn't I?

Clearing my throat, I tapped on the counter with my keys. "Yeah, I'm going to need two pairs of shoes. A size seven and a …?" I glanced back at Gabriel. "What size do you think you wear?"

Gabriel peeked down at his feet and shrugged. "I don't know. I just think of it, and it appears. Not really a size thing."

Oh, the jokes I could tell. Swallowing my ill-timed humor, I glanced toward the cashier who was giving me a strange look.

"Well, take your shoe off and let me see it." I held my hand out to him, hoping to get a guesti-mate from the woman behind the counter.

Gabriel didn't do what I asked and rubbed the back of his neck bashfully. "I can't."

"Why not?"

"Because I'm not corporeal. The clothes aren't real."

His answer baffled me for a moment, and then when it finally clicked in my head, my mouth dropped open. I slowly turned back to the counter where the woman stared at me like I was some kind of crazy person. Chuckling nervously, I clacked my keys on the counter once more.

"Just a second." I marched away from the counter and toward the bathrooms. Forcing myself to ignore the stares coming my way, I ducked behind the row of lockers. When Gabriel stopped behind me, I scowled. "Why didn't you tell me? I looked like an idiot talking to myself."

Gabriel shrugged. "I forgot until you mentioned my shoes. It's not like I go corporeal every day."

"Well, you might as well get used to it because I can't have my boyfriends going all invisible at random." I waved a hand up and down him before digging into my bag.

"Your boyfriends?"

My hand in my bag, I glanced up at him for a second and said, "Yeah, Michael and I already had this discussion, so I assumed he told you." Ducking my head back down, I searched for the nail file I knew I'd thrown in there earlier.

"It must have slipped his mind because this is the first I'm hearing of it." Gabriel tipped his head down until I looked up. The silly grin on his lips made me smile.

"Is that okay?" I asked and then winced as the nail file broke the skin in my hand. I offered it up to him.

Gabriel leaned down and lapped at my hand, his eyes on mine the entire time. Soaked. My panties were completely destroyed. It wasn't fair really. He was an angel. How was I supposed to be able to resist public arousal with him nearby?

The moment Gabriel became corporeal, his arms wrapped around my waist and drew me to him. His mouth closed over mine, and for a moment, I forgot why we were even hiding. My hands gripped his button-down plaid shirt, a thankful change from the Hawaiian shirts he'd been favoring as of late.

A gasp and giggle interrupted us, and I pulled back to see two ten-year-old boys staring at us. Blushing, I wiped the sides of my mouth. Gabriel, on the other hand, didn't seem at all affected by their presence.

"Are you dating him?" one of the boys asked, raising an eyebrow.

Before I could answer, Gabriel did. "Yes, this is my girlfriend, Jane. And who are you?"

"Ryan," the boy answered and then nodded to the other boy. "This is my friend, Charlie. Are you going to kiss again?"

Gabriel grinned at the boys and wrapped his arm around my shoulders, tugging me into the junction of his arm. "I just might."

The two made a face that could only be described as a mixture of disgust and curiosity. Somebody hadn't figured out that cooties were a good thing. Give them a few years.

Not wanting to play twenty questions, I gave Gabriel a little shove. "Well, we have to go get our shoes. It was nice meeting you. Don't do drugs and stay in school. You know all that good stuff."

Dragging a laughing Gabriel away, I reminded myself to renew my birth control. We stopped before the counter once more, and the cashier arched a brow.

"I'm back." I grinned awkwardly.

"I see that." She clucked her tongue and jerked her chin toward Gabriel. "Found your friend, did ya?"

Feeling even more awkward, I turned back to Gabriel and patted him on the chest, grinning way more than needed. "Yep. Found him. Hey, Gabriel, give me your shoe."

Gabriel took his shoe off and handed it to me. The smirk on his lips told me he was enjoying this way too much.

"Can you size this for me?" I slapped the shoe on the counter.

The woman looked down at the shoe and then back at me. "You don't know the size?"

"They're custom made," I bit out.

The woman rolled her eyes and took the shoe and went to the shoe rack. She grabbed a pair off the rack and then another pair before coming back over. Slapping them on the counter, she gestured to them. "There. Your boyfriend's an eleven." She wagged her brows at Gabriel and winked. "Lucky girl."

Now, I was really blushing. I dug into my pocket and pulled out a twenty. "Here, thanks." Grabbing our shoes, I hustled Gabriel away from the counter.

"So, you're lucky, huh?" Gabriel chuckled, tucking his hands into his pockets.

I rolled my eyes. "Don't get a big head. It's a stupid joke that doesn't mean anything."

"Well, it sure meant something to her." Gabriel pointed back at the woman at the counter, who hadn't stopped staring at him. *That's right, lady, he's mine. Back off!*

Finding an empty lane, I sat down and started changing my shoes. "Yeah, well, the only people who care are really immature people." I glanced up from my shoes and saw the women still openly staring. "Geez, look at this woman. You'd think she'd never seen a hot guy before. Freaking snotty ho face."

Gabriel snorted.

Once we both had our shoes on, I took Gabriel over to the ball rack. Gabriel picked up the first ball he found, not at all bothered by the weight. I searched the rack for the bright pink ball that I knew weighed nothing and wouldn't rip my arm off. I found it three racks over and had to jog for it before a little kid could get it.

"That's right, kid. Keep moving!"

Gabriel stared at me curiously, but I ignored it and headed for the lane. "Alright, let's bowl. You have bowled before, right? They have lanes in Heaven."

"What?" Gabriel asked, confusion furrowing his brow.

"You know." I waved a hand in the air. "That whole tale that says when thunder sounds, God and the Devil are bowling, and when there's lightning, that means they hit a strike." I felt my lips spreading out across my face as I realized how that sounded. Lucifer? Bowling?

Gabriel let out a mixture of a scoff and a laugh. "Yeah, right. Like Lucifer would ever wear these shoes."

"It's like we are of one mind!" I gasped, gesturing between us and giggled.

Picking his ball up, Gabriel glanced at the holes. "So, I just stick my fingers in here, right?"

"Yeah," I moved over to him and showed him

how to put his fingers in the holes, something he never needed help with in the bedroom. I held back my snicker.

"And then I just throw it down that strip of wood?" He gestured the ball toward the lane, and I backed off a bit.

"Woah there, you're gonna hit someone if you don't watch it." I held my hands up, trying to get him to lower the ball.

"Sorry," Gabriel put the ball to his side. "So, what are you going to do about the thief?"

I palmed my ball and chewed on my lower lip. "I'm not sure. Mandy and O'Connor seem pretty dead set on arresting the maid."

"Yeah, but we both know she didn't do it." Gabriel moved up to the line of the lane. He glanced at some of the other bowlers and then rolled the ball down the lane. His form was perfect, and he got a strike.

"What the hell?" I gaped, coming up beside him. "You said you'd never bowled before."

Gabriel shrugged. "I haven't."

I pursed my lips. "Uh huh." Moving up to the line, I aimed my ball at the pins. Come on, strike. I couldn't get outplayed by an angel on his first time!

Fucking spare!

Growling, I stomped back over to Gabriel. "Even if we know she didn't do it, I doubt Detective I'm-always-right will listen to reason. Not until they've torn the place apart. What we need is the M.E. to say suffocation. Then we might have a chance."

Gabriel picked up his ball and moved up to the line again. "Well, I think it's a waste of time but whatever. They're the experts."

I made a disgusted noise in the back of my throat. "Yeah, the experts. That's why they hired a fake psychic to help them in this case."

Giving me a knowing look, Gabriel threw the ball down the lane. Once more, perfect form and a … a strike. Damn it!

We played that way for a few more rounds before I threw in the towel. I should have never tried to play a game with an angel.

"I swear this is not fair." I sighed, hanging forward with my ball dejectedly. "It took me years to get a semi-good game, then you come in here with your angel moves and mastered it in five minutes."

Coming over to me, Gabriel placed his hands on either shoulder. "Don't worry. There are plenty of things I'm not good at."

My head jerked back, and my eyes narrowed. "Like what?"

Gabriel was quiet for a moment, and then his eyes widened slightly. "I can't tell if someone's lying automatically."

I gave him a perturbed look. "Really? You're playing off Lucifer's powers now?"

"Hey, I'm also not very observant." He lowered his head a bit so that we were eye level.

"That doesn't count either." I pushed away from him and sat my ball down on the chair near us. Sitting down next to it, I leaned over on my knees. "I'm sorry, I don't mean to be such a sore loser."

"Oh, it's okay." Gabriel sat down beside me and wrapped an arm around my shoulders. "I don't mean to be good at everything. It just goes with the package." He gestured down at his body. His toned, sculpted body, that had me thinking about balls in a whole other way.

Licking my lips, I snuggled in closer to him. "What do you say that after this, we go back to my apartment, and you can show me what else you're good at?"

Gabriel jumped to his feet. "How about now?"

I giggled and pointed at the lane. "We're not

even done with our game. I thought you wanted to play?"

Grabbing my hand, Gabriel waved his other behind him. "Nah, I win either way you look at it, and between bowling and sex, I'd rather have sex."

I didn't need to be psychic to figure that out.

20

When I parked my car outside of my apartment, I didn't bother waiting until we were inside before leaning over and kissing Gabriel. His hands came up, cupping my face between them. Smiling into the kiss, I climbed out of my seat and into Gabriel's lap.

"What are you doing?" Gabriel asked, breaking our kiss.

Licking my lips, I began to unbutton his shirt. "Making out with my boyfriend in the parking lot." I adjusted myself so that I pressed up against him, giving him a wicked grin.

Gabriel grinned wolfishly as I rocked against him before pulling my face back down to his. I continued to unbutton his shirt, making a small sound in the back of my throat as my fingers found skin. I trailed down his chest and to the waist of his pants. Gabriel's breath hitched as I played with the button of his pants.

His hand caught mine before I could unsnap them. "Maybe we should move this up to your bed."

I pulled away from him with a curious grin. "Are you shy? Afraid of getting caught with your pants down in public?"

Meeting my gaze, Gabriel laced his fingers with mine. "More like I'm already barely fitting into your tiny car, and I'd like room to appreciate you more."

Giggling, I leaned over and grabbed my bag and the keys out of the ignition. "Alright, you win. The bed it is."

We scrambled out of the car and made our way up the stairs to my apartment, our hands never leaving each other. Gabriel stopped me and pushed me up against the wall beside my apartment door. His mouth pressed against the side of my neck, his fingers tugging at the belt loops of my pants. I tangled my hands in his hair, pulling him closer to me. I was so caught up with Gabriel that I didn't hear my neighbor open her door.

"Excuse me." Mrs. Branch, a sixty-year-old

senior citizen with way too much time on her hands, snarled.

My eyes fluttered open, and I met her disgusted gaze. Tapping a hand on Gabriel's shoulder, I pushed him away slightly. "I'm sorry, Mrs. Branch. Did we wake you?"

Mrs. Branch sniffed. "I may be old, but I'm not that old. Your canoodling is interrupting my show. Take it inside."

"Sorry, Mrs. Branch." I grinned and fumbled for my keys. "Won't happen again."

"See that it doesn't," she snapped, slamming her door behind her.

Gabriel and I exchanged a look before we busted out laughing. Finally getting the door open, I threw my bag and keys down and turned back to Gabriel who was on me in seconds. I gave into his kiss for a few moments before pushing him away with a grin.

This time, I didn't waste a second getting his pants off and then knelt before him. His cock stood hard before me, bumping against my lips. My tongue dipped out, and I took a long, languid taste of him, enjoying the sounds he made from above. As I pulled him into my mouth, his fingers laced into my hair, urging me closer.

My finger gripped the back of his legs as I took him inside, moving my mouth along his shaft. Before I could get too far into it though, Gabriel pulled me to my feet. I gave him a questioning look as his hands went to my shirt.

"I want to see you too, you know." He pulled my shirt over my head, and I helped him take my bra off. Our mouths collided once more, and we backed up toward my bed. When my legs hit the bed, he unsnapped my pants but didn't take them off. His hand dipped into my pants stroking me over my panties. I let out a shuddering breath, and my eyes fluttered closed.

"You're so beautiful, Jane," Gabriel breathed out against the side of my face, his hand moving fast against my pulsating clit.

I groaned, arching into his touch. "So are you."

Gabriel chuckled. "I'm beautiful?"

My eyes snapped open, and I grinned. "Well, you are an angel. Beautiful is kind of your thing."

"No, you're my thing." Gabriel removed his hand, making me whine in protest, but I was soon pacified when he shoved my pants off. Urging me back onto the bed, Gabriel hovered over me, his eyes taking in my nude form. "I don't think I'll ever be able to get enough of seeing you like this. Of touching you." His hand slid along the underside of my breast. "Of tasting you." He ducked his head down to press an open mouth kiss to the same breast. "I never want to leave you."

"Then don't," I gasped, his mouth taking my nipple in.

Gabriel rolled the tip around in his mouth for a moment before pulling back. He moved up to my face and brushed his lips against mine, his hand reached between us and lined the head of his cock with my entrance. "You have no idea how much I wish that were an option."

I didn't get a chance to ask him about what he meant before he pushed inside of me. We rocked together, our hands and mouth finding any skin we could. There was no more talking, only the steady beating of our hearts as we each searched for our release. My nails dug into Gabriel's back, and my back curved up. The action made Gabriel slide into me a bit deeper, and suddenly, I didn't need to reach for my orgasm. We broke over that edge close together, and I couldn't think of anything but how good I felt. I had already forgotten about Gabriel's words and was able to fall into a deep, restful sleep.

The next morning, like so many other mornings before, I woke to the annoying sound of my phone.

I groaned and rolled over in bed. My hand reached out for Gabriel, but as usual, he was gone. One of these days I planned to wake up with the same person I went to bed with.

I collapsed back on the bed once more, hoping whoever was paging me would take the hint and leave me alone. Sadly, just as I started to fall back asleep, my phone started to ring again.

"Damn it!" I shouted to the empty room and threw the covers off me. Why couldn't I remember to turn my phone off before I go to bed? Oh, that's right, I was a bit preoccupied with a certain angel and his hands down my pants.

Not at all bothered by the fact that I was walking through my apartment naked, I snatched up my phone. Mandy, of course. Only she would be so heartless to call me this early in the morning.

"This better be good," I answered, putting the phone between my ear and the shoulder. I went over to the fridge and opened it. Slim pickings there. I grabbed a box of leftover pizza from three nights ago before the whole case went down.

"We got the report back from the medical examiner," Mandy said as I threw a piece of pizza in the microwave. "What are you doing?"

"Making breakfast."

Mandy made a disgusted noise. "It's almost noon. Are you just getting up?"

Leaning against the counter, I snorted. "More like you woke me up."

She sighed. I could imagine the look on her face. Her utter disapproval clear in that one sound. "You shouldn't stay out late when we have a pending investigation. It's not very responsible."

This time I had to laugh. "Says the woman who was nursing a hangover just last night."

There was a pause, and then Mandy said, "That was different. I was keeping you from doing something stupid."

"Like getting drunk in my hotel room alone?" The microwave dinged. I pulled the pizza out and shoved half of it into my mouth. "Hot! Fuck!" I said my words all garbled from the food.

"That'll teach you," Mandy sniffed. "In any case, you and Gabriel were right. Ernie died of suffocation, and Crystal has an alibi for the time frame we have for the time of death."

"Oh really?" I took another bite of my pizza and chewed as I thought about what she said. It wasn't surprising that Gabriel had been right or that Crystal had an alibi. Gabriel had said she didn't look like the killer. The problem was, if she didn't kill Ernie, then who did?

"Yeah, Crystal was at some employee party the night he supposedly died. She had half a dozen witnesses to corroborate her story."

My eyes widened. "Oh, I was at that party with Michael. Well, for a few minutes anyway. Then you called, and I came down to see you at the station. That's where I'd learned about Ernie and Crystal."

"Did you see either of them at the party?"

"No." I lifted myself up and sat on the counter. "I searched around but didn't see either of them. Then again, we didn't stay around that long. She could have come and gone at any time."

"Still, we don't have anything on her to keep her much longer. If we don't find something, we'll have to let her go soon." Mandy let out a heavy breath. "I just want this case to be over. Not like I don't have enough on my plate as it is."

"Still fighting with the FBI?" I asked, finishing off my breakfast. When Michael showed up out of nowhere, I almost choked on it.

"Jane? Are you alright?" Mandy's concerned voice called over the phone.

Coughing, I got the piece out of my throat and swallowed hard. Hopping off the counter, I glared at Michael before answering Mandy, "Yeah, I'm fine. Just about died is all."

"Remember to chew before you swallow, Jane," Mandy chastised.

"I'll remember that," I told her, my eyes firmly on Michael. "I've got to go, I'll call you if I find anything out."

"Okay, but we should really think of a p—" I cut her off before she could finish her sentence and sat the phone down.

"Michael," I drew out, holding my phone in one hand and leaning my hip against the counter. "You're here early." Then I remembered the time. "Or I guess it's not that early. I'm just late."

The archangel was quiet as he took in my nude form not leering but inquisitive. "It seems you had a nice time last night."

"Yes, I did." I moved away from the counter and over to the end of the bed where I kept my pile of clean clothes. "For once, no one interrupted us." I shot him a warning look.

Michael made a face. "That was entirely not my fault. There was a problem that had to be taken care of."

"And the hand of God couldn't deal with it on his own? He needed the Devil to help?" I asked, pulling a shirt over my head and then digging for a pair of bottoms.

"It was a team effort kind of problem," Michael explained, his eyes moving over my legs as I pulled on my panties. "As I recall, our date was cut short as well."

I scoffed. "It was paused not cut short. We finished it later in my room." I pointed a finger at him with a smirk. "You just like to pull Lucifer's chain."

"I'm not sure about what chain you speak of, but Lucifer could use being knocked down a peg or two. He can be quite big-headed." Michael had moved closer now. If he were corporeal, we could almost touch.

"Like you're one to talk." I smiled up at him. "Save Gabriel, you two all think mighty high of yourselves."

Michael's hand brushed against the side of my face causing me to jolt a bit at the sensation. "I wouldn't think so highly of Gabriel. He can be just as high and mighty as the rest of us. Especially when it comes to you."

I flushed and bit my lower lip. "Well, I'm flattered." Turning away from him, I grabbed a pair of shorts and pulled them on. "So, to what do I owe this pleasure?"

"I heard from Gabriel that there was now a killer on the loose instead of just a burglary. I wanted to make sure you were okay." Michael crossed his hands over his chest and looked me over. "It seems like you are in one piece."

"For now." I winked and headed over to my bag where I'd tossed it last night. "I'm heading to meet Mandy now. Hopefully, we can get to catch the burglar and the killer all in one go. I have a feeling they are one and the same person."

"Then I'll accompany you." Michael approached me from behind. "Though I hate to ask, I will need to be solid if I am to be of any use."

Grinning, I pulled out the same nail file from last night. "Oh, I could think of a few things you could be useful for."

21

I texted Mandy to find out where she was and was surprised to find out she was at the spa. Redirecting my car toward the spa again, I filled Michael in on where we were going.

"I don't understand." Michael frowned his eyes on the dash. "If they already arrested the person they think did it, why are we going back?"

"Because Crystal didn't do it. She has an alibi and witnesses. Plus, Gabriel had a vision. It wasn't her." I pursed my lips and tried to think of what Mandy had planned. They'd already made me check out so coming back here wasn't going to help. I couldn't just check back in and act like nothing happened.

We were quiet while I drove the rest of the way to

the spa. This time I wasn't as giddy to arrive as the first time. Of course, that could be the fact that I wasn't going to relax and spend the taxpayers' money. I was going to find and catch a killer. At least, I hoped.

I parked the car and got out, directing Michael to follow me. I shot a text to Mandy letting her know we were here. I found her in the lobby waiting for me. Alone.

Frowning, I glanced back at Michael who didn't seem to know what was going on either.

As we approached her, she turned to me. Her eyes went to Michael, but she didn't comment on it. "I'm glad you're here. I had an idea that we haven't tried yet."

"An idea?" My eyebrows shot up in surprise. "Like what? Wave a sign and shout, 'Are you the killer?'"

Mandy gave me an incredulous look. "No. You said that Gabriel had a vision of the killer. Well, maybe the killer and the thief are the same person. If they were wearing dark clothes, maybe they were robbing a room when Ernie found them. It could explain his sudden death."

I clucked my tongue and then nodded. "Yeah, that sounds pretty plausible. I had sort of the same idea. Except without the whole 'catching him in the act' bit. So, how do we catch our thief-slash-murderer?"

A wicked grin covered Mandy's lips. "That's where you come in. Or well, you." She pointed at Michael.

"Wait? What?" I asked, placing a hand on Michael's arm. "What about Michael?"

"Well, your cover is already blown. Everyone has seen you and think you worked here. So, we're going to send someone else in." She eyed Michael with a grin. "Someone no one will suspect of being part of the police department."

"You're forgetting, Michael was my date at the staff party. The whole room saw him with me. I'm sure they'll figure it out." I crossed my arms over my chest and felt like stomping my foot. No way was I letting my best friend put my boyfriend in the line of fire.

"It's fine, Jane." Michael touched my arm, his eyes soft. "I doubt anyone will remember me. I'm sure whatever Amanda has planned will work."

Chewing on my lower lip, I wanted to argue, but we didn't have any other options at the moment. Besides, I didn't even know her plan yet. It probably wouldn't be anything bad. It'd be fine. Right?

"Come on." Mandy waved us down the guest hallway. "I reserved two adjoining rooms under two different aliases, of course. Not even the manager knows who rented them."

She opened the first room which had a bunch of surveillance equipment set up. There was even a monitor showing another room on the screen.

"So, you plan on spying on them?" I asked, sitting down on the couch in front of the monitor. "How's that going to catch the thief?"

Mandy shook her head, her blonde ponytail bobbing behind her. "No. I mean yes. The plan is to have Michael go around talking about the fact that he has something really expensive in the safe in his room. That way it draws the thief's attention." She sat next to me and pointed to the screen. "I have cameras set up in the room we are going to pretend is his. That way, when the thief comes to steal it, we'll have him on camera."

"How do you know the thief will even hear me talking about it?" Michael asked, sitting on the arm of the chair.

I pointed a thumb at him. "That's a good point,

or even if the thief will come today. Maybe they don't show up until tomorrow. Or whatnot."

Mandy held a finger up. "Ah, I thought of that. The thief always stole from guests who were only staying one night. So, I made sure to book the room for the same time frame. If the thief wants to get the prize, then he will have to do it today."

I reached out and tried to adjust the camera screen, but Mandy smacked my hand. Glaring at her, I rubbed it. "How do you know he'll come today? Maybe he'll wait until tonight to do it."

"Because the thief knows the guests will be out during the day," Michael explained before Mandy could. "It is a spa, correct? They will be at the beach or getting a massage. It would be easy for the thief to know where you are."

"Especially if they worked here," I added, beaming up at him. "We make such a good team."

Michael smiled back at me. Mandy cleared her throat, interrupting our moment. "As I was saying. We already had suspicions that the thief was part of the staff. It was the only way to explain the ease of access to the items and being able to break into the safes without knowing the codes. Obviously, I would have pinned that on the security guard but since he's …"

"Dead," I supplied.

"Yeah, that." Mandy frowned before standing. "Since Ernie is no longer in the picture, it couldn't have been him, or if it was then, he had a partner."

"I don't think so." Michael shook his head. "This doesn't seem like a two-person job, and if it were, why kill this Ernie character now?"

"Exactly." Mandy's brows furrowed. "I'm surprised you figured that out without all the information."

I placed my hand on top of Michael's and grinned. "Well, he is the hand of God for a reason." I couldn't help the pride in my voice.

"It's a bit more than that, but yes, my position does make it easier for me to see the big picture and to find those facts that others miss." Michael squeezed my hand in return, a soft smile on his lips.

We were quiet for a moment, and then Mandy clapped her hands together. "Alright, then. We might as well get this show on the road." I started to stand, but Mandy stopped me. "No, Jane. It's best if you stay in here. We wouldn't want someone to recognize you and know we're still investigating. I'm going to stay in here, as well, after I tell Michael what to do."

Pressing my lips together tightly, I refrained

from arguing. Mature of me, I know. While Mandy talked to Michael, I tried to wrap my head around the plan. The idea of Michael going out into the human world all on his own bothered me. I'd been holding him and the others' hands this whole time. It almost felt like I was unnecessary, like they could handle themselves. Which I supposed they could. They were angels after all. If anyone could deal with humans, it would be them.

"Do you think you have it?" Mandy asked, drawing my attention. "Go to the lobby. The dining room. Anywhere there are a lot of people and make a lot of noise about proposing to your girlfriend and that the ring is in the safe in your room."

"Understood." He nodded and then gave me a sideways glance. "I'll be sure to make my intentions loud and clear."

My mouth went dry at his words. His intentions? What were his intentions? Suddenly, it wasn't about the thief anymore but about us. Michael didn't expect to one day marry me, did he? Could he even do that? I didn't find the idea horrifying. Though I couldn't imagine marrying one of them and not the rest of them. The country wasn't quite that accepting of alternative lifestyles yet.

I could just imagine how that would go. "Hello,

I'm Jane, and these are my brother-husbands. Also, they're angels!" Yep, we could have our own reality T.V. show. Or a room in the insane asylum.

In any case, we weren't even close to ready for that kind of commitment. At least, I wasn't. We'd only been able to really have a relationship in the last few weeks, though I wasn't sure that doing it at every opportunity classified as a relationship. Sure, we'd started going on dates, but I think we needed a few more uninterrupted dates to constitute a serious relationship. Calling them my boyfriends was a big enough step as far as I was concerned.

"Jane," Michael said, a bemused look on his face, "are you alright?"

I cleared my throat and shook my head. "No, no. I'm fine. Just got a bit lost in thought is all. Are you ready?"

"I'm prepared." He answered simply, but then sat down beside me. "Are you sure you're alright with this? I don't have to do it, you know."

Sighing, I placed his hand on mine. "I know, but we need you and like you said, you'll be fine. If anyone can catch this guy, it'll be you." I paused for a moment, my tongue wetting my lips. "Just … just don't do anything heroic okay? You're solid now, and we know that means you can get hurt. I don't want anything to happen to you."

Michael reached up and brushed my hair away from my face. "I'll be alright. I hardly doubt the scrawny person Gabriel saw will be able to overcome me."

"But what if he has a gun?" I asked, my heart suddenly starting to race. "Or a knife? Sure, hand-to-hand, you are the bigger person ... angel ... thing, but that doesn't matter if he shoots you."

Wrapping an arm around my waist, Michael dragged me into his lap. "Don't worry. I'll be careful. I won't do anything rash and will come back to you as soon as I can." He pressed his mouth to mine in a quick but passionate kiss that left me breathless and not a bit less concerned.

However, before I could protest, Michael stood and left, leaving me alone with Mandy. Taking the seat beside me, Mandy patted my leg. "Don't worry, he'll be fine. Plus, all he's doing is spreading the word, not confronting the thief head on. He has clear instructions to come back here after he tells everyone he sees about the ring. Then we'll watch from here for the thief."

I nodded. I heard the words coming from her mouth, but they didn't make me feel any better. Just because Michael wasn't going into the room, it didn't mean that the thief wouldn't try something with Michael. Maybe they steal the room key from their victim first. If they weren't part of the maid's group, how else would they get in?

My mind reeled with all the possibilities. It only got worse as time went on. A minute turned into five and then half an hour. Before long, it had been an hour, and still, Michael wasn't back yet. I had long since left the couch and started to pace the floor. Mandy stood a small distance from me on the phone with O'Connor.

"I'll be back in shortly. Yes, we're taking care of it." Mandy crossed an arm over the other and sighed. "No, you don't need to come down here. We're fine. You just keep working on Crystal. We still have time until you have to let her go."

I waved at her, trying to get her attention. Mandy glanced my way and held a finger up.

"No, it's fine. I'll call for back up if I need it." Mandy nodded. "I promise. Okay, I have to go. Bye." Mandy hung up the phone. "I swear, that O'Connor. He's worse than my mother. You'd think that he'd trust me to run this operation."

"He's just concerned, I'm sure," I quickly said and then stepped toward her, my arms hugging myself. "Shouldn't he be back by now? Should we go look for him?"

"No." Mandy put her hands on my arms. "We can't go out there right now. I'm sure he's just doing a thorough job. He'll be back soon."

I started to ask her how the hell did she know but there was a knock on the door. My feet moved beneath me on their own, urgency causing their pace to quicken. I glanced in the peephole briefly, and Michael's distorted face greeted me. I jerked open the door and pulled him inside, hugging him to me.

"I'm alright." Michael hugged me in return, his hand stroking up and down my back.

"I was so worried." I sagged into his embrace. "I thought you were never coming back."

Michael shut the door and brought us further into the room. "My apologies, I got stopped by a rather talkative group of women. I had a hard time getting away from them with my shirt."

"Did you do it?" Mandy asked, not at all concerned about his wellbeing.

I frowned. "Give him a chance to catch his breath before you start interrogating him. Jeez."

Michael pressed his lips to my cheek and grinned before turning to Mandy. "It's done. I doubt there is a single person in the spa who doesn't know about the ring."

"Good." Mandy nodded and went over to the couch.

"Now what?" I asked, clinging to Michael as if he might disappear at any moment. Which he just might. They had a bad habit of that.

Mandy adjusted something on the computer and looked up at me. "Now. We wait."

22

Apparently waiting was a typical thing for Mandy to do on the job. I'd always imagined if they were waiting for a bad guy it was, like, BOOM, breaking down doors and yelling. Didn't criminals have common courtesy for those of us with other things to do?

My stomach grumbled. Lunch. That sounded like something hugely important right now. I'd already missed breakfast in my hurry to get over here.

"How much longer?" I asked Mandy, who was checking the computer again for any activity. Nothing had changed.

Mandy lifted a shoulder. "I don't know. It could take all day. We don't really have a time frame."

I groaned and leaned back on the couch. I wish Michael were still here. He had to leave for something or another an hour ago. My eye caught sight of the mini fridge. Inching off the couch, as casual as can be, I started for it. I glanced over at Mandy, whose back was turned to me, before kneeling by the fridge. I put my hand on the door.

"No." Mandy's stern voice made me freeze, my shoulders shooting up to my ears. "No mini fridge."

"But Mandy," I whined, standing up and stomping toward her, "I'm starving over here."

Mandy shot me a look. "I don't know how you stay in such good shape with how much food you shove in your pie hole."

"Oh, pie," I cried out longingly, pulling at my hair. "And it's just good genetics."

Mandy snorted. "Sure. Too bad those genetics don't apply to your patience."

I leaned against the back of the couch and poked at her back. "That has nothing to do with it. Any sane person would be going crazy sitting in a room with nothing to do but scratch her ass."

"Please don't do that." Mandy made a disgusted face. "And you can have one thing from the fridge. One." She held her finger up just as I started skipping to the fridge.

My hand reached for the mini bottles of alcohol and Mandy added, "No alcohol."

"Why not? This party needs a bit livening up." I held up two bottles of tequila and shook my tits at her.

Giggling, Mandy shook her head. "This isn't a party, and it's not even after five yet."

I shrugged. "So, when has that ever stopped us before?"

Mandy leveled a glare at me. "No, absolutely not. We can get good and drunk after we catch this guy." She turned back to the computer and waved a hand over her shoulder. "Get something food wise out of there and get back here. We don't want to miss anything."

Sighing, I went back to the fridge and grabbed a bag of chips. Glancing at the price tag, I winced. Ten bucks for potato chips? What, were they made by blind Tibetan monks? They better be some holy potatoes was all I could say.

Flopping back onto the couch, I opened my chips and glared into the bag.

"You look angry. Are you really that hungry? Or did the chips hurt your feelings?" Mandy asked, not looking away from the computer.

"Look at this bullshit." I held the bag out to her, so she could see the inside.

She glanced away from the computer screen quickly before turning back to it. "What about it?"

"Ten bucks for one, two, three, eight chips! Eight fucking chips and the rest of the bag was air. What a fucking rip-off." I shoved my hand into the bag and grabbed a few of the chips. Putting them in my mouth, I chewed them around before swallowing. "And they taste like a fridge. I'm paying ten dollars for fridge chips."

"Oh God, Jane, can you be any more dramatic?" Mandy shot me an incredulous look which quickly turned to alarm as something moved on her screen. "This is it! Look."

Tossing my chips aside, I leaned toward her, my eyes on the screen. Something was moving on one of the cameras. "Are they coming through the window?" I gaped at the screen.

Mandy frowned. "It does look that way." We watched as the person in a pair of dark pants and a sweatshirt with the hood pulled up over their head started into the room. They kept their head down as they went straight to the built-in safe.

"It's the window washer!" I pointed at the screen. "How come you didn't put him on the list of suspects?" The memory of the window washer platform sitting outside the spa when I first arrived came to my mind. They must have been spying on me when I first stayed here.

"We didn't know about him. The manager never said anything about him." Mandy grabbed her gun and badge and stood. "Come on, let's get in there before he sees there's no ring."

I got up and started after her but stopped her at the door. "What about O'Connor? He said to call him for backup. We can't go in there by ourselves."

Mandy pursed her lips. "The guy is barely half my size, soaking wet. I don't think we need any backup."

"What if he has a gun?" I asked, digging my fingers into her arm. On my list of things to do before I died, getting shot was not one of them.

"I have a gun too, you know." She placed her hand on her holster. "Now, are you coming, or you waiting in here?" She shook her head. "Actually, you wait here. I'll take care of this."

"The hell you are," I shouted, chasing after her and into the hallway. We inched toward the door next to ours, and I whispered, "Are you going to kick it down? Maybe shoot the lock off?" I held onto her shoulders, using her as a shield. Hey, a girl had to think about her own safety. And Mandy had a gun!

Digging into her pocket, Mandy pulled out a card. "I'm going to use the key. Really, Jane. You watch too much television." She slipped the key into the door slot and shoved it open. The door banged against the wall as Mandy hurried inside, her gun at the ready.

A crash followed by a set of pounding feet alerted us that the thief had heard us. I shoved at Mandy's back. "He's going to get away. Hurry up!"

Mandy glared at me before running into the room. "Freeze, police! Stop, or I'll shoot." She pointed her gun at the dark figure, who kept his head down so we couldn't see his face. Her shout only made the thief move faster as he darted for the window.

Panic raced through me, and I searched for something to throw. Mandy tried to get a good shot while I grabbed the nearest thing to us, a coffee pot. Running into the bedroom, I chucked it with all my might. It banged into the thief's head just as he tried to escape through the window, causing him to lose his balance and fall onto the platform.

"Score!" I shouted, hopping in place as I fist bumped the sky.

Mandy rushed up to the window, but the impact of the thief falling had caused the platform's lock to break, sending the contraption falling to the ground. I stopped celebrating and ran over to the window beside Mandy.

"Is he dead?" I asked Mandy, who put her gun up.

"No, it's only a two-story building. Come on." She pulled me away from the window. "We need to get down there before he wakes up and has a chance to bolt."

She pulled her phone out and hit her speed dial. "Yeah, it's me. We caught the culprit. It was the window washer. We're heading to make the arrest now." She paused for a moment as we hurried down the stairs. Who had time to wait for an elevator? "Okay, see you in a few."

"That O'Connor?" I pulled the door open to the stairwell and stumbled into the lobby.

"Yeah, he'll be here shortly." Mandy put her hand on her gun as she searched for an entrance to the back of the building.

I pointed to an emergency exit next to the stairwell. "There. We can get out that way."

Mandy nodded and pushed the door, causing a blaring alarm to shout through the lobby. Wincing at the sound, I raced after her, not wanting to miss a thing.

We moved around the building until we saw the window washer's platform where it had smashed into the ground. Thankfully, as we came up to it, there was still a prone figure laying inside of it.

"Now, what?" I asked her as we stared down at the figure.

Mandy frowned. "Well, he seems out cold. We have to wake him up before we can arrest him."

"So, more waiting?" I asked, but before Mandy could answer, I kicked the guy in the side. He groaned and shifted atop the collapsed platform. "Look, he's waking up."

Glaring at me, Mandy pointed her gun at the guy and then dug out her handcuffs. "Here, since you're in such a hurry. Why don't you cuff him?"

I glanced at the cuffs and then back to the guy who had rolled over, his hood falling back. "Riley Parks!" I cried out, pointing a finger at the weaselly-looking manager. "I told you it was the manager, but nooo, no one listens to me." I beamed at Mandy who only shoved the cuffs into my hands.

I clutched the cuffs as I approached him, his eyes finally coming into focus. He tried to scurry away from me, but I jumped on top of him. "Now, hold up. I didn't wait all this time for you to get away."

"Get off me." Riley twisted beneath me, trying to fight the cuffs.

"Riley Parks," Mandy moved into his line of vision, so he could see the gun. "You are under arrest for the multiple thefts here at the Blessed Falls Spa Resort as well as the murder of Ernie Slousky. You have the right to remain silent …"

"Fuck you!" Riley snapped as I clipped the handcuffs on him.

I smacked him on the back of the head. "Hey, that's my best friend you're talking to. Have some respect."

"Screw you, you mumbo jumbo bitch."

I glanced up at Mandy. "Do you have to arrest him? We have a gun. We could just end it right here."

Mandy gave me a disapproving look. "No. Now can you hold him down until O'Connor and the others get here?"

I bounced on top of Riley slightly, making him groan. "No problem. Maybe I can teach him the weight of his actions."

"The only weight I'm feeling is from your big ass. Get off me. This is police brutality, I'll sue!"

He shot Mandy a glare, and I bounced a bit more.

"Hey, I'm not that heavy, and I'm not a cop. So, chill." Riley grumbled under his breath but didn't fight me any longer. "You know, to pass the time, you could tell us why you would call the cops if you're the one stealing stuff."

Riley glowered up at me. "I'm not saying crap without my lawyer."

Of course, he wasn't. "Well, I bet I could guess. Then you could tell me if I was right or wrong?"

Mandy tapped on the platform's railings with her gun. "Stop antagonizing him."

"I'm not." I squinted up at her, the sun getting into my eyes. "I'm helping you do a thorough job."

Mandy rolled her eyes and dialed her phone. Probably calling O'Connor to ask him where the hell he was.

I turned my attention back to Riley. "So, you got this big idea to steal from your guests. You use the window washing platform to spy on the guests to see if they were in their rooms. Then when they were gone, you'd go into their room and steal from the safe."

Riley grunted beneath me, not agreeing or denying it.

I continued, "I bet Ernie figured it out and tried to catch you in the act, just like us. That's when you smothered him with one of the pillows from the room and then stashed him in the fridge while everyone was at the big staff party."

"You don't know what you're talking about," Riley growled, shifting beneath me. "Why would I want to kill Ernie?"

I leaned forward a bit. "Maybe because he was now dating your ex-girlfriend and you know how much of a mooch he was. But sadly, Crystal doesn't know how much of a cold-blooded killer you are. You'll never get her back now."

"I did it for her!" Riley shouted, finally breaking. "She wanted to leave Ernie, but he had taken out all this debt under her name. I was only trying to help her."

"Thanks for painting such a clear picture for us," O'Connor said as he and a couple officers showed. They came over to me and grabbed Riley so that I could get up.

I smirked and wiped my hands on my pants. "Just doing my job."

"Not you," O'Connor frowned at me. He turned to Mandy and asked, "How did he get the safes open?"

"Haven't you ever forgotten the password to one of those hotel safes?" Mandy put her gun in her holster and faced him. "Usually, you have to call the manager to get it open again. I'm assuming that's what happened."

"Yeah, what she said." I threw my arm over Mandy's shoulders and grinned.

"Well, good job, Stevenson." O'Connor jerked his head toward her and then stared at me. "Mehr." The last bit was like an afterthought as he followed the officers back inside with Riley Parks in tow.

I patted Mandy on the shoulder. "So, ready for some tequila?"

Mandy cocked her head at me before shaking it. Walking away from me, I held my hands out. "What? You said after we're done. It's after!"

23

I followed Mandy and the others back to the police station in my car. Except I stopped at Macho Del Taco on the way. A girl's gotta eat!

Pulling into the parking lot of the police station, I tossed my empty wrapper in the passenger seat and got out. With my stomach full, I hoped I would get paid today. I wanted to add this case's payment to the already bulky amount I'd gotten from Mrs. Garret's ghost. It would make things a lot easier if I didn't have to worry about money for a while.

I walked through the parking lot, calculating my bills, my eyes on the ground … and stepped right through something that caused my whole body to tingle. More than familiar with the buzz of walking through an angel, I turned to gripe at whichever one of the guys decided to mess with me.

My words caught in my throat when I came face to face with someone I didn't know. He had dark eyes almost to the point where his pupil swallowed the iris. His equally dark hair was long and hung around his shoulders. Unlike my angels, this one didn't bother trying to pass as human. He wore long dark robes with intricate designs, his feet bare.

"Uh, hello?" I cocked my head to the side and adjusted my bag on my shoulder. "I don't think we've been introduced. I'm Jane."

The angel was quiet for a moment, his eyes going over me the same way I'd done. Except he didn't seem nearly as impressed.

Getting uncomfortable with his staring and not speaking, I shifted away from him. "Ohhhkay. I'm going to go now. It was nice meeting you, whoever you are."

I turned away from him and started toward the police station, but then he spoke, his voice low and commanding. A bit like Michael's really. "So, it is true. You can see us, human."

Pursing my lips, I spun around. "Yes, I can see you, and I can hear you. By the way, it's not human. It's Jane. J-a-n-e. I don't know how they do it up there." I jutted a finger toward the sky. "But down here, it's polite to use someone's name."

The angel didn't seem at all affected by my ranting. In fact, he only seemed mildly curious. Taking a few steps toward me, the angel crossed his hands behind his back.

"I will address you as you are. A human. One of many bugs that infect this planet." His nose curled up in clear disgust. Someone was prejudiced.

"If humans disgust you so much, then why are you here?" I snapped, putting my hands on my hips. This guy was really starting to get on my nerves.

The angel's eyes flashed with anger. "Do not address me in such a manner, human. You are nothing but a flea compared to the rest of the universe. How Michael has taken such a liking to you is beyond me. Gabriel and Lucifer, I could see, but you are far below the likes of Michael. I suggest you keep your distance if you value your pathetic life."

I started to argue that my life was far from pathetic, but he had disappeared. Growling in frustration, I stomped my foot and spun on my heel. Freaking angels and their stupid superiority complexes. Seriously, it's not like I wanted to see them. They're the ones who kept coming to me, not the other way around.

Of course, that's how it had been at the start. Now, I was more than happy to see my angels. Well, not that particular angel. He could keep his asshole self as far away from me as possible.

I shoved the police station door open and found Smith sitting at her desk. Great. Just what I didn't want to deal with.

Coming up to her desk, I tapped my fingers on the counter to get her attention. "I'm in a bit of a hurry. Could you buzz me back?"

Smith looked up from the magazine she was ready to look at me. "No, I can't just buzz you back. What kind of place do you think this is? The courthouse?" she waved a hand with long red painted nails toward the bench. "You can go sit over there and wait for the detective to come get you."

"But I don't have time for this," I argued, gritting my teeth.

"And I don't have time for your sass. Now, do as I say, or you can wait in a holding cell." She raised a brow at me.

I wasn't sure she could actually throw me in jail, but I didn't want to take the risk. Huffing my displeasure, I shuffled over to the bench. Sitting down next to a painted-up woman in a short sparkly purple dress, I forced a smile. "I like your dress."

"Thanks, honey." The voice that answered me was low and masculine. It made me do a double take on the woman. By the time Mandy came to get me, I was deep in discussion with Tanya about what kind of skin care she used to keep her looking so young and feminine.

"Jane?" Mandy grinned at me as I exchanged numbers with Tanya. Never hurts to make new friends, especially ones with fabulous fashion sense.

"Gotta go." I hopped off the bench and waved at Tanya.

"See you, girl. And don't forget to moisturize."

"I won't!"

Mandy chuckled as she let me in the back. "Well, you make friends fast."

I shrugged. "People just like me, I can't help it." We went into the conference room where O'Connor stood. He glanced up from his papers and glared at me.

Mandy patted me on the shoulder. "Sure, they do."

"What are you doing here?" O'Connor snapped, his hands on his hips, a bit too close to his gun for my comfort. "The case is closed. Shouldn't you be out chasing someone's cat or summoning the spirit of someone's granny?"

I crossed my arms over my chest. "I'll have you know that I don't find pets. I have allergies. Also, summoning spirits takes a lot of work. There are passports involved, and you need a special kind of candle you can only get from India in the fall."

"Right," O'Connor drew out, baring his teeth to me like he might bite his own tongue off for asking.

"And I'm here to get paid and help you out on your murder case." I reached for the file in front of him, but he jerked it away from me.

"You're not qualified to help in this case," O'Connor told me with a nasty grin.

I cocked my hip to the side and smiled. "Actually, I think I am. It was me who figured it out it was the manager from the beginning, and if you'd only listened to me, we would have just had a robbery and not a murder."

"Well, I—"

"And she did find the dead body," Mandy jumped in, pointing a finger at O'Connor. "And she managed to make him reveal so much that he was forced to sign a confession."

O'Connor stared at Mandy like he wanted to rip her head off before scowling and shoving the file toward me. "Fine, but if you die on the job, that's on you."

I picked up the file a satisfied grin on my lips. "Thanks, I'll keep that in mind. I'll just take this home with me to look over."

"No, you can't take—"

I didn't wait for him to tell me no but darted out of the conference room and toward the payment counter. Today was just getting better and better, if you didn't count the encounter with the asshole angel.

"Hello, Bernadette," I greeted the lovely lady at the counter, who I knew would write me a check. Bernadette was a large blonde woman who didn't fit her name. No one with arms that toned could possibly be called Bernadette. She should be tiny and have a small cute voice, maybe even glasses. But not Bernadette. She could probably even take on O'Connor and win.

"Jane, how are you?" Bernadette greeted me, putting her green protein shake concoction down on the counter.

"I'm good." I beamed at her. "You're looking quite buff as per usual."

"Thank you!" She flexed her arms and puffed up her chest. "I have been lifting more lately. Are you here for a check?"

"Yep," I nodded. "I helped with the Resort robberies."

"Oh, I heard about that! You helped catch a thief and a killer. Good job." She pulled out the packet of checks and started to scribble on one of them.

When she didn't fill in the amount, I frowned. She turned to a file and searched for something before she started typing away on her calculator. After she was done, she filled in the check with a number way lower than I had thought it would be.

Ripping it off the pad, she handed it to me. "Here you go, Jane."

I squinted at the check, hoping I was reading it wrong. "Are you sure this is right? It's way less than I got last time."

Bernadette glanced at the file she had and then back to me with a frown. "Yes, that's what they have. Your consulting fee, minus the expenses you racked up at the resort."

"Expenses!" I shouted and then ducked my head and lowered my voice. "What expenses? Everything should have been paid for."

Shaking her head sadly, Bernadette showed me the file. "They covered the room and meals but all this extra stuff here, they said I'm not allowed to cover. They weren't pertinent to the job."

Glaring down at the file, I saw the massage I had gotten, the charges to the mini fridge from my and Mandy's night of drinking. If I'd known they weren't going to pay for any of it, I wouldn't have gotten that massage. Who knew getting rubbed down cost so much?

Oh yeah, I did. That was why I wanted the police to pay for it. I pouted to myself.

I bet this was O'Connor's doing. It sounded like something that jerk face would do. He didn't want anyone else to have fun because he was grumpy about getting divorced. I'd like to get him in a room by himself for a few minutes. Handcuffed to the table of course. He was a big guy.

With thoughts of torture and pain in my head, I had half a mind to go back there and give O'Connor a piece of my mind. However, I'd have to stay here with the file, and I didn't want to do that. I wanted to be in my own bed without pants for the rest of the day. Preferably with a sexy angel in my bed.

Handing the file back to Bernadette, I sighed. "Thanks. Just a misunderstanding."

"Alright." Bernadette took the file and offered me a small smile. "At least, you caught the bad guy."

"Yeah," I forced a smile. "I'll see you later."

Leaving the counter, I shoved the check in my purse and started for the door. I caught sight of O'Connor who had a shit eating grin on his face but didn't stop me from leaving. If he thought he could get to me, then he had another thing coming.

I walked out the door separating the Lobby from the back, my eyes immediately going to Smith. She gave me an I'm-watching-you look that made me shiver. Thankfully, Tanya was still there to cheer me up. I waved at her with a grin. I wouldn't let O'Connor ruin my day with his penny-pinching.

Leaving the station, I headed to my car. I had a check to deposit and some pants to get rid of. Maybe I should take a shower? That usually made them show up unannounced. Before I could even get out of the parking lot my phone went off.

An unknown number showed up. "Hello, this is Jane."

"Jane Mehr from Gotcha?" a male voice asked.

"Yes, this is she."

"We had reports of electrical fluctuations in your area and need you to come down and let us in to take a look." The moment he said, electrical fluctuations I had a feeling I knew what had happened.

Freaking angels.

"Alright, I'll be right there." I hung up the phone and turned my car toward the office. I guess going pantsless would have to wait.

24

When I arrived at Gotcha!, the lights were flickering, and a crowd had begun to form around the front of the building. Unbeknownst to them, I could see the angels inside having a shouting match.

I scrambled from my car and headed for the door. Before I could get to it, I was stopped by a man wearing a polo shirt and slacks. The logo on his shirt told me he was from the local electric company.

"Miss? Are you Jane Mehr?" he asked, gesturing to the building. "The owner of this building?"

"Yes, that's me."

"Well, we're going to need to get in there to check the breaker box. Everything out here seems fine. No broken lines. Nothing to indicate why your electricity should be freaking out like that." He nodded toward the dancing lights.

"Of course," I agreed and fumbled for my keys. Putting it in the lock, I turned it and allowed the electrician to go first before following after him. My eyes immediately went to the angels who hadn't stopped arguing.

"You know we have to tell her," Gabriel said firmly. "She needs to know."

"No, she doesn't." Michael shook his head. "It will only cause unneeded panic."

"Oh, so what are you going to do when he shows up?" Lucifer scoffed, crossing his arms over his chest.

"Miss?"

My head jerked away from the arguing angels to the electrician. "Huh?"

"I asked if you had any overfilled power strips, or if you left any appliances on?" He gestured around the office. His questions apparently were enough to make the angels realize they had an audience and quickly clammed up.

"No." I shook my head, distracted by their conversation. "Nothing like that."

Of course, as soon as they stopped fighting, the

lighting quit going crazy. The electrician looked up at the ceiling and snorted. "Isn't that always the way? The moment we get here, it stops."

"Yeah, that is something else," I politely agreed, my eyes on the three angels who were avoiding my gaze. The fact that they hadn't disappeared right then surprised me, but then again, they probably knew it would only make them get in more trouble. And they were already in heaps.

The electrician stared down at a clipboard he had brought in with him and then back to the room. "Well, I'm going to check the breaker anyway. Better safe than sorry."

"Sure, that's fine. It's back there." I pointed toward the kitchenette area, more than happy to get him out of the room. Once he was gone, I moved over the front window of Gotcha! and closed the drapes. No need to have an audience for this one.

"So, who's going to start?" I asked, standing in front of the three of them. Michael opened his mouth, and I held a hand up to stop him. "How about someone who wasn't planning on lying to me?"

"We weren't going to lie to you," Lucifer said, glancing at the other two. "We were just going to omit what was going on."

"Like that's so much better," Gabriel scoffed.

Shaking my head, I tapped my foot. "Really, Lucifer, I'm surprised at you. You're the lie detector, and you were planning on lying to me?" He started to correct me, but I stopped him. "Omit, fine. Same difference."

"We're sorry." Gabriel moved over to me, an apologetic look on his face. "We've been wanting to tell you about this for a few days now but haven't found the right time to do it."

"Tell me what?" I tensed, afraid of what they might say.

"There's other—"

"Gabriel," Michael snapped, cutting him off. "She doesn't need to know. It's taken care of."

"That doesn't mean she doesn't have the right to know." Lucifer pointed a finger a Michael. "That way in case you haven't taken care of it, she's not caught unaware."

I was really getting tired of all the cryptic talk. "Someone just tell me what's going on?"

The answer I got wasn't from the angels but from the electrician. "Well, it looks like everything is fine as far as your breaker goes, but you really should get someone in here to update it to the newer model. They save you so much more money."

He walked through the guys without a single notion that they were there. He tapped his clipboard and then handed it to me with his pen. "Can you just sign this saying I came by and checked it out?"

"Sure." I took the pen from him and scribbled my name on the line he pointed to. "Anything else you need?"

"Nope." He smiled and nodded his head. "Have a good day and let me know if you have any other troubles."

"Will do." I waited for the electrician to leave before going behind him and locking the door. Spinning on my heel, I marched back over to the guys. "Start talking."

Michael sighed and held up a hand so the others would let him talk. "There's nothing to worry about."

"If there were nothing to worry about, then you wouldn't have kept it a secret," I countered, already tired of this conversation.

"Very well, you are correct." Michael inclined his head, unease showing in his eyes. "We kept this from you because we didn't want you to—"

"Freak out," Gabriel supplied.

Michael frowned at him. "Yes, freak out."

"Well, keeping it from me isn't going to make

me freak out any less. Especially if I have to find out from someone else." I shot them a warning look.

"Hey, don't look at me." Lucifer held his hands up. "I've wanted to tell you from the beginning. It's Mr. I'm-the-one-in-charge who didn't want to."

"That's not exactly how I said it." Michael glared at Lucifer.

Fed up with all the back and forth, I threw my hands up in the air. "Okay, enough of this whose fault it is. Just tell me what the big secret is."

Before Michael could get another word out, Gabriel jumped in. "Other angels are looking for you!"

My face scrunched up in confusion. "Huh?"

"What Gabriel so eloquently said." Michael stared at the other angel, who stared right back at him. "It has come to our attention that other angels have found out about you and your particular … abilities."

"What he means to say is that Gabriel went around bragging about all the sex he's been having to all the other angels." Lucifer smirked, completely at ease about throwing Gabriel under the bus.

I gaped at Gabriel. "Really, Gabe? I'd expect it from Lucifer, but you?" I tut-tutted and shook my head. "I'm so disappointed."

Gabriel rubbed the back of his neck, a shameless grin on his lips. "What can I say? I was excited. Besides, it wasn't just the sex. I told them about bowling and the hot sauce. All of it."

"Yeah, so now that big mouth let the Jane out of the bag," - Lucifer pursed his lips in irritation - "they are looking for you, because they want to have a chance to be human as well."

"Well, that's not so bad." I shrugged my shoulders. "I mean, I'm not saying I'd do it all the time, but I don't know why you wouldn't want them to try it out too. Unless they are expecting me to have sex with them." I cocked a brow at them. "They aren't, are they?"

"No," Gabriel shook his head. "Not at all. We made it very clear that you were not available to any of them."

"I hear a 'but' coming on." I shifted my weight from one foot to the other.

"But they might ask anyway," Lucifer said.

Michael glowered at Lucifer. "No, they won't. This is just a warning to be careful."

Suddenly, I remembered the asshole angel in the parking lot. With a small voice, I asked, "One of those angels wouldn't happen to dress in dark robes with shoulder-length black hair and have a stick up his ass, would he?"

"Uriel," Michael immediately answered. "And yes, he's one of those who knows about you. Have you seen him?"

"Obviously." Lucifer snorted. "She wouldn't know what he looked like if she hadn't."

"What'd he say?" Gabriel asked, worry in his voice.

I shrugged and moved over to my desk to sit down. "Nothing much, just some crap about how he didn't see what you guys saw in me. That he thought Michael was above all that. Also, he doesn't like humans, like at all."

Michael sighed and ran a hand over his face. "I was afraid of that."

"Why? What's wrong?" I leaned forward in my seat, anxiety starting to fill me.

Shaking his head, Michael approached the desk. "I don't know, but I'm not sure how I feel about other angels wanting you. Not that I can blame you. This is a temptation I'm not sure any of them will be able to resist."

I swallowed thickly. "And by the temptation, you mean me, right?"

Lucifer chuckled, his eyes darting up and down

my form. "Oh, yes. You are quite the temptation, love."

"Oh."

"Oh is right." Michael's eyes narrowed at me, a serious tone filling his voice. "I want you to promise me that if you see him again, you will call for us. Right away. Don't chit chat or do your usual pain in the ass routine. Right away."

I scoffed and shifted in my seat. "What pain in the ass routine? I'll have you know, I am a hundred percent natural. I don't practice any of my quips."

Gabriel and Lucifer chuckled behind Michael.

When Michael didn't laugh, I sighed. "Fine. I promise. No assholery from me. I'll call for you right away."

"Good." He started to turn away, but I wasn't having any of that disappearing crap. I had reparations to be paid.

"Hold up a second," I snapped. "I promised to call for you, but that doesn't fix the fact that you lied to me. I demand payment for your misdeeds."

"Misdeeds?" Michael arched a brow. "For wanting to ensure your safety?"

I snorted. "Trust a man to think he's keeping a woman safe by keeping her out of the loop. No, sir. Not this girl. If I'm in this mess because of you guys, then I get to know everything. Which means, I get to ask something of you." I grinned wickedly at all three of the angels who had a mixture of expressions ranging from intrigue to horror.

"What would you like, love? Just name it." Lucifer purred, coming closer to me. I knew where his mind was going, and for once, mine was lining up with the Devil's.

"Did I ever tell you guys about this dream I had where all four of us were going at it?" I grinned as Lucifer and Michael paled. "It was really great except that my mom showed up in the middle trying to force feed me pizza. But I think we should put that on the table. The group sex, not the pizza part. Though, I really think I could go for some right now."

Laughing to myself, I grabbed my phone and dialed the pizza place. The guys started to argue with each other about my suggestion. I kicked back in my chair and grinned happily. I had solved the case, established my agency as a liaison to the police, gotten myself a line of work for the future, and got to do it all with three drop-dead-gorgeous men at my side and in my bed. In a world where angels existed, it really did pay to be the only one who saw them.

THANK YOU FOR READING!

Curious about what happens to Jane, Michael, Lucifer, and Gabriel next?

Find out soon!

AUTHOR'S NOTE

Dear reader, if you REALLY want to read the next Her Angels novel- I've got a bit of bad news for you.

Unfortunately, **Amazon will not tell you when the next comes out.**

You'll probably never know about my next books, and you'll be left wondering what happened to Jane and the gang. That's rather terrible.

There is good news though! There are three ways you can find out when the next book is published:

1) You join our mailing list by clicking here.

2) You can also follow Erin on her Facebook Page. We always announce new books in those places as well as interact with fans.

3) You follow us on Amazon. You can do this by going to the store page (or clicking this link) and clicking on the Follow button that is under the author picture on the left side.

If you follow me, Amazon will send you an email when I publish a book. You'll just have to make sure you check the emails they send.

Doing any of these, or all three for best results, will ensure you find out about my next book when it is published.

If you don't, Amazon will never tell you about my next release. Please take a few seconds to do one of these so that you'll be able to join Jane and the gang on their next adventure.